Art

Catt Chasin'

JUL 2011

CH

Catt Chasin'

Shana Burton

www.urbanchristianonline.net

Urban Books, LLC
78 East Industry Court
Deer Park, NY 11729

ISBN 13: 978-1-60162-791-9
ISBN 10: 1-60162-791-2

First Printing July 2011
Printed in the United States of America

10 9 8 7 6 5 4 3 2 1

Distributed by Kensington Corp.
Submit Wholesale Orders to:
Kensington Publishing Corp.
C/O Penguin Group (USA) Inc.
Attention: Order Processing
405 Murray Hill Parkway
East Rutherford, NJ 07073-2316
Phone: 1-800-526-0275
Fax: 1-800-227-9604

CATT CHASIN'

By Shana Burton

Dedication

This book is dedicated to the wonderful men in my life who have been my friends, brothers, handymen, lunch providers, book hustlers, confidants, and, in a few cases, my significant other: Adrick Ingram, Demetrius Hollis, Damon Wilson, Brian Harmon, Manuel Johnson, Anthony Richards, Scott Harris, Quinterrence Bell, Davarious Lamar, and Phillip Lockett.

It is especially dedicated to my good friend and favorite Nupe, James "Jimmy" Lunsford, Jr., who inspired my male protagonist, Jamal Ford, and to Dwarka Jackson, who brought my heart out of its hiding place.

Acknowledgments

Before I acknowledge anyone, I must acknowledge and give thanks to God, who is the joy and the strength of my life. Without Him, I have nothing. With Him, I have everything. To Him be all the glory forever and ever. God has given me the gift to write and opportunity to do what I love while ministering to other people. More important, He placed so many wonderful people in my life, which is more than I could have ever hoped for. If you are listed on these next two pages, please know that I thank God for you all the time. I pray that God will use me to be the same kind of blessing to you that you have been to me.

I would like to thank my boys, Shannon and Trey, for being the best kids ever! You are my heart, and you have kept me going during my darkest moments. The two of you are the kindest, most talented, brilliant, resilient, handsome, loving, and fun people I've ever met. I love you more than you'll ever know.

Thank you to my mother, Myrtice C. Johnson, who never fails to love and support me unconditionally. I don't know what I did to be worthy of a mother like you, but I thank God for you every single day. I love you so much! Thank you to my father, James L. Johnson, for being my sounding board and friend. Thank you for never prying! I love you. I hope you know that.

Thank you to my sister, Myrja, and my brothers, Jay and Matthew, for your love and support. I especially

Acknowledgments

want to thank my brother Jay for starting a book club, convincing the members to read my book, then disbanding the club. That's gangsta! Love ya, boo!

Many thanks go to my best friend and play-sister Deirdre Neeley. Aside from the Lord and my mama, I don't think I've ever had a more loyal friend. Thanks for all the times you loaned me your couch, a listening ear, and unsolicited advice. More than that, you introduced me to Nikki and Lola, for which I will always be grateful. Nothing compares to having a friend who will have your back, even when you're wrong. Thank you for always being there.

Thank you to all of the book clubs, bloggers, bibliophiles, and reviewers who have supported me, whether it was from my debut novel or my latest release. If it wasn't for you getting the word out about my books, the only one reading them would be my mama! A supersized thank you goes to Ty Moody, Ella Curry, Urban-Reviews, Chocolate City, Black Expressions® Book Club, Raw Sistaz, APOOO, OOSA, All the Buzz Reviews, Christian Fiction Blogspot, Chick Lit Gurrl, Books A Latte, Christian Bookworm Reviews, Arms of a Sister, Joey Pickney, Dreams 4 More Radio, Bella Online, The Unique Reviewer, Shelfari, Divas Read 2, Books & Beauty, Victorious Café, Chapters of Conversation Book Club, Positive Minds Book Club, Book Remarks, Wanda B. Campbell, Tiffany Warren, Rhonda McKnight, Ashea Goldson, Curled Up With a Good Book and a Cup of Tea, LaShaunda Hoffman, Cyrus Webb, Words of Inspiration Book Club, Tamika Newhouse, Romance in Color, Sisterhood Book Club, Anjuelle Floyd, Sherrell Valdezloqui, Literary Gumbo, This That and the Other Thing, The Coupon Sista, Nubian Lit, Simply Said Reading Accessories, Loving Heart Mommy, Macon State College, Morehouse Col-

Acknowledgments

lege, Virginia College, and a host of other people who I can't think of at the moment, but know that I love and appreciate you!

I would be remiss if I didn't acknowledge my awesome writers' group, The Writer's Voice, and all of its members: Brian, Traci, Van, Rena, Keisa, Della, and Lady T. To members Nicole Ingram and C. Lindsey Pennimon, your support has been nothing short of amazing. You all are my sisters, and I love you so much! I also have the best Facebook friends, and I sincerely thank all 2,500 of you for your support and well wishes, especially ride-or-die chick, Yolanda Gore.

Thank you so much to my publicist Dee Stewart. You have been extra patient with me, and you've become so much more to me than a publicist. I consider you to be a friend. Thank you to my editor, Joylynn Jossel. There was hardly any bloodshed this time; I must be getting better!

Thank you to my Northeast family for continuing to support me, especially Becky Ehalt, for always keeping my books in stock, and to Aaliyah James and Yocasta DeJesus for keeping me motivated all of those days on the road. Thank you to my Beulahland Bible Church family for continuing to buy books out of my trunk after church and sending me those encouraging and uplifting e-mails.

To Dwarka Jackson: There are some people who change your life forever. You're one of those people. "I was fumbling around in the dark. Then God turned on the light, and there you were." I'll tell you the rest when I see you . . .

Last, but not least, thank you, loyal reader and book supporter! Thank you for taking time out of your day and money out of your budget to spend with me. I hope

Acknowledgments

you think it was well worth the effort. This is my promise to you: If you keep on reading 'em, I'll keep on writing 'em! Much love . . . be blessed and be a blessing.

Chapter 1

Jamal Ford only ordered a glass of water and calamari that night. There was no point in ordering anything heavy; he knew how the evening would end before they even set foot in the restaurant. It was 8:12 P.M.
when they arrived and by 9:00, he'd be at home, catching whatever was left of the Lakers game. He'd already
decided that twenty minutes into dinner, he would of-
fend her, start an argument, then drop his blazer off
at the cleaners on the way home because she would
predictably saturate his suit with wine, tea, or whatever beverage was close at hand before storming out.
He could only hope that she'd grab his drink instead of
hers as her weapon of choice. After all, it was a $300
sports coat. A little water wouldn't hurt it too much.

It was Day fifteen, and Patrice Luke had made it to
the crucial halfway point without even knowing it. For
the unsuspecting Patrice, the third Tuesday in March
simply marked her fifth date with Jamal Ford, the
handsome head of cosmetic research and development she'd been dating for the past two weeks. To Jamal, however, it wasn't just the third Tuesday in the
third month of a new year; it was the midpoint of his
thirty-Day Plan, a dating guide that he had created for
himself to weed out the scalawags, drama queens, baby
mamas, and gold diggers.

Jamal met Patrice while having a drink at The Blue,
a trendy bar in Charlotte, North Carolina, the city he'd

called home for the past six years. He'd gone to The Blue that day to celebrate being named the new head of Research and Development at Telegenic, an up-and-coming minority-owned cosmetic company. It was a definite pay cut, but offered a much-needed change of pace and a real opportunity to make his mark in the cosmetic world. Jamal quickly decided that physical gratification was a more attractive alternative to the evitable amaretto-and gin-induced hangover when Patrice with her curvy legs and supple figure sashayed through the door. While there was no real escape from the sting of losing money, he could take comfort in temporary, yet beautiful, distractions like his jazz collection and Patrice Luke.

So far, Patrice had fared pretty well on her basic tests. The half-Black, half-Dominican stunner had excelled in the looks department. She was twenty-seven, had no kids, and had never been married—all pluses in Jamal's mental notebook. Although she was a college dropout, she did manage to meet his minimal requirements for intellect, grace, and ability to hold a conversation. Ordinarily, her questionable job status as an aspiring model practicing secretary would have immediately eliminated her as a serious contender for his heart, but after she scored an audition for a supporting role in a Tyler Perry film, he'd decided to keep her around. She wasn't too much in the kitchen but made up for it with skills in the bedroom. She had been well on her way to taking the top spot on his "team" when she made a fundamental mistake: she suggested that he take her to Aquavina for dinner.

The problem wasn't that he couldn't afford an upscale dining experience. His nearly six-figure salary made sure of that. The problem was that *she* couldn't afford one. Considering that this made the third restaurant she'd recommended that was out of her price range, Jamal concluded that it was time to officially take Patrice off "person-of-interest" status and place her squarely on "gold-digger watch." Gold diggers, like insects and rodents, would not be tolerated, and by the end of the night, both he and his bank account would be rid of Patrice.

Jamal checked his watch. It was 8:32. He cleared his throat and drove his plan into action.

"I have a friend I want you to meet," he said casually as the waiter set their orders down in from of them.

"Oh," replied Patrice and took a sip from her glass of Cabernet. "Is he someone from work?"

"No, *she's* an old friend from college."

Patrice raised an eyebrow. "*She?*"

Jamal laughed. "Don't worry, she's cool. I think you'll like her."

She rolled her eyes, then muttered, "If you say so."

"I do. Tamara is great. She's smart, funny, and sexy as all get-out. I think you two would really hit it off."

"I don't really get along well with too many females, Jamal," she snapped. "I thought I told you that."

He nodded. "You did, but she'll only be in town for a few days. Since she's staying at my place, I thought you should meet her. I don't want things to be awkward while she's here."

Patrice's eyes widened. "Did I just hear you say that she's staying with you?"

He frowned. "You don't expect me to send her to a hotel, do you?"

"That depends." Patrice crossed her arms. "Where is she sleeping?"

Jamal smiled a little. "With me, of course."

"*With you!*" spat Patrice.

Jamal reached out and caressed her hand. "I'm sorry, baby . . . with *us*."

Patrice's mouth flew open, and she snatched her hand back. *"What?"*

"Yeah, what's the problem?" It took every ounce of strength he had to keep a straight face.

Patrice stared at Jamal in total disbelief. "Are you kidding me?" she fired.

He smirked and pushed his calamari around on his plate. "Come on, Patrice. Don't act like you've never indulged in a threesome. You're in the entertainment industry. Do you honestly expect me to believe that you haven't engaged in a few extracurricular activities to land a role or an audition?"

Patrice squinted her eyes. Jamal could almost see the blood rushing to her face. "Excuse me?" she hissed.

"See, there you go, getting an attitude." He shrugged his shoulders. "What's the big deal?"

"The big deal is that you just basically called me a prostitute and insinuated that I would be willing to sleep with you and another woman!" she raged, pointing a finger at him.

Jamal remained cool. He knew that doing so would rile her even more. "Well, it's not like you would be the first girlfriend I've ever had to be open to that sort of thing. Honestly, sweetheart, with you being an actress and all, I just assumed that you dabbled in a little porn from time-to-time to help make ends meet or to get your foot in the door with certain producers or agents. I didn't think that adding Tamara to the mix would be a far stretch from what you already do."

"Just what kind of woman do you think I am?" shrieked Patrice and bolted from her seat.

"Clearly not the kind who's down for a little ménage à trios," mumbled Jamal, looking down at his plate.

When Patrice spied the bewildered looks from eavesdropping strangers, she sat down and regained her composure. She took a deep breath. "We seem to be having some sort of disconnect here," she stated calmly. "Suffice it to say, I don't do threesomes, and it's definitely *not* okay with me that you're going to have this woman living with you."

Jamal leaned back in his chair. "I don't think it's your call to make, Patrice. I wasn't asking your permission. I was just giving you the heads-up."

"You know what—" Patrice fumed and flung her napkin on the table. "I think I just lost my appetite. Take me home."

"Why? You've barely touched your food."

She reached for her purse and cell phone. "Are you going to take me home, or do I need to call someone to come get me?"

Jamal sighed and shook his head. He pulled out his credit card, more than happy to pay the bill and send Patrice on her merry gold-digging, hyperemotional way. "You're overreacting, you know that, right?"

"I'm *what?*" she snarled.

"Overreacting," he repeated and signaled to their waiter. "Not to mention being childish and petty."

Patrice rose again, visibly agitated. "You know, maybe we need to take a break for a couple of days and give each other time to reflect on whether this relationship is worth pursuing. We seem to have *very* different ideas about what's acceptable and what's not."

"So now you want to break up, huh?" Jamal shook his head. "So typical. I thought you were different, Patrice. If I had known that you would flip out on me like this, I never would've . . ." He sighed, preparing to bring out the big guns. He stealthily edged his glass of water closer to her reach. If at all possible, he really wanted to avoid that wine stain on his jacket.

"Never would've *what?*" demanded Patrice, anchoring her hands on her hips.

Jamal looked up at her with his deep, honey-colored eyes brimming with sincerity. "I never would've told Adam about you."

"Who's Adam?" she cried.

"Patrice, Adam was my first love and has never stopped being my lover. A threesome with another woman is no big deal, but if I invite Adam to join our bed, it means that you're someone I could be serious about. I would only share him with a woman I cared for very deeply."

Patrice froze in horror, as if the world had stopped spinning. This scenario was all too familiar. Jamal began counting down and braced himself. If the slap or the drink in the face didn't come when he mentioned "Tamara," it came—without fail—whenever he brought up his fictitious lover, Adam, usually within five . . . four . . . three . . . two . . . one.

Right on cue, Patrice called him a sick bastard and followed up with the proverbial glass in the face before telling him to lose her number and storming out in a dramatic fashion. As fate would have it, she reached for the Cabernet.

Jamal blotted the stain off of his jacket, more upset about the damage done to his attire than the damage done to his relationship. He promptly began contemplating which female currently sitting on the bench would be promoted to Patrice's now-vacant spot. But that was a matter he could settle in the morning. For now, he had to drop off the jacket before the cleaners closed at nine and, of course, there was a game to catch.

Chapter 2

Pastor Jeremiah Cason looked up from his Bible long enough to gaze lovingly at the framed picture on his desk in his church office. He couldn't help but smile at the snaggletoothed little girl and the beautiful woman who grinned back at him.

The woman in the picture was Ola, his wife and soul mate, who had gone home to be with the Lord ten years earlier. The little girl, his daughter Catt, was now the spitting image of her mother. Catherine, known as Catt by most, had blossomed into a brilliant, caring woman, who'd traded her pigtails for a chic haircut and her dolls for a bachelor's and master's degree in chemistry.

With his beloved wife gone, Jeremiah devoted his life to two things: continuing to win souls for God's Kingdom and his only begotten child. He'd promised Ola that he'd look after their daughter and make sure that she never lacked anything she needed. He rested easily at night knowing that he'd been able to keep that promise. Jeremiah made sure that Catt successfully made it through college and graduate school debt free. He helped her move into her first apartment and was at her side when she closed on her two-story ranch-style home. He coached her for her first big job interview and pled the blood of Jesus over her every day and every night.

Where he had not been so successful was in making sure that Catt had a life outside of the cosmetic lab, where she worked. Jeremiah had envisioned running around with his grandkids and going to football games with his son-in-law by this point in life. Instead, all he had was a few reassuring *"I'm still young, Daddy! There's plenty of time for that"* speeches from Catt.

Jeremiah sighed and wiped the lenses of his glasses. He knew what the problem was. They all did. While Catt was cute, she wasn't what the average man would consider sexy. She was a beautiful, sweet woman of God, but she was also a very *full-figured* woman. Jeremiah worried that men would be so focused on her weight that they would overlook all of her other wonderful qualities. Whenever he mentioned his concern to Catt, her response was always the same: "That's their loss, not mine!" But in reality, it was both of their losses.

Jeremiah was resolute and determined that there was nothing his daughter would lack, including a man who loved her as much as he did. After careful prayer and consideration, he found a solution to both of their dilemmas through unassuming and spiritually minded thirty-three-year-old Minister Eldon James.

There was a knock at the pastor's door, followed by Eldon, who ducked to slip his head through a crack in the door. "You wanted to see me, Pastor?"

Jeremiah nodded. "Yes, come in, son."

Eldon came in and closed the door behind him. "I have the proposal for the youth lock-in right here." He placed the folder on Jeremiah's desk. "Everyone else has signed off on it. All we need now is your signature."

Jeremiah flipped through the folder, nodding at times, then scrawled his signature across the last page. "Excellent work, Minister! I think one of the best decisions I ever made was putting you in charge of the youth ministry."

Eldon grinned. "Well, thank you, sir. It's an honor for me to serve God and the congregation here at Faith Temple."

"We're blessed to have you. I think very highly of you, son. I hope you know that."

"Thank you. I'll try to be worthy."

"You know, Catt thinks highly of you too," added Jeremiah with a twinkle in his eye.

Eldon smiled sheepishly. "Your daughter is a very special woman."

"That she is, but she works too hard. I guess she gets that from me," admitted Jeremiah. "But even I know there's more to life than work. It's been on my mind a lot these days."

Eldon sat down in a chair across from the pastor. "What has?"

"Retiring, handing over the reins to someone a bit younger, stronger. I can't do this forever. I'm not even sure that I want to try."

"But, sir, you *are* Faith Temple Worship Center," asserted Eldon.

"No, son, God is. I'm just one of His many stewards." He noted the look of concern registered on Eldon's face. "Don't worry—I don't plan on going anywhere any time soon. But I'll be fifty-three this year. I'm not the same man I was when Ola and I came here almost thirty years ago. The bottom line is that we've got to be able to attract young people, particularly young families. Sometimes it takes a younger pastor to do that."

"I can't imagine anyone else leading the congregation but you."

"Well, I have my eye on someone," he hedged. "He's a man of great character and integrity who loves the Lord. Plus, he's young enough to draw in some young folks but stable enough to keep the church going. He's also the man I'm hoping will be my son-in-law one day."

Eldon let out a breath. "That's a tall order!"

"I'm sure he can handle it." Jeremiah reeled back in his chair and folded his hands over his protruding belly. "Tell me, Eldon, what do you think about my daughter?"

Eldon smiled. "She's one in a million. She's going to make some lucky man very happy one day."

"I've watched the two of you interact with each other. You're quite smitten with her, aren't you?" Eldon lowered his head, embarrassed. "It's okay," shared Jeremiah with a chuckle. "I'm not going to drag you out behind the church and beat your brains out."

Eldon's anxiety dissipated. "Catt is the kind of woman I've been praying for my whole life," he disclosed. "Unfortunately, I don't think she has a lot of room in her life for a man right now."

Jeremiah nodded. "Yeah, I know. She won't leave that lab long enough to meet anybody. I hate to see her making that job and this church her whole life."

"All you can do is pray for her, sir."

"I do, but faith without works is dead. Sometimes we have help those we love see what they're missing." He stood up and walked over to Eldon, resting a hand on his shoulder. "I've watched you for a while now. I know that you're a righteous man of God; there ain't too many of y'all out there these days, especially not your age."

Eldon shook his head to decline the compliment. "Don't go putting me on a pedestal, Pastor. I'm still human. As they say, I'm not sinless; I just try to sin *less*."

"Nobody expects you to be perfect, but the fact that you're not too proud to admit that you have weaknesses says a lot about your character." Jeremiah returned to his seat and held up his worn Bible. "You know, Timothy says that an overseer should be a man who is 'above reproach, temperate, self-controlled, respectable, hospitable, able to teach . . ." Jeremiah turned to I Timothy in his NIV Bible and read aloud. "He must not be a recent convert, or he may become conceited and fall under the same judgment as the devil. He must also have a good reputation with outsiders, so that he will not fall into disgrace and into the devil's trap." He closed the book. "Now I think those are mighty fine traits to have, not only in a pastor, but also in a husband. At least the kind of husband I want for my angel. I believe you fit the bill, son."

Eldon was humbled. "You see all that in me, sir?"

"If I didn't, we wouldn't be having this conversation," Jeremiah told him.

"I know how much you love your daughter. It means a lot that you would trust me with her heart, not to mention taking over here once you retire."

"You've proven yourself to me and to this congregation. When the time is right and with a little more training and experience, I think you'd be the perfect person to take over the helm."

"It's a huge honor and responsibility and one that I want you to know I don't take lightly." He leaned into Jeremiah. "I don't talk about this with a lot of people, but I think this church is primed to be the next megachurch for folks in the South."

"Really?" replied Jeremiah, surprised.

"Yes, sir. God has given me a vision for this church. I see us doing all kinds of outreach ministries, opening up a school, and making a lasting change in this city." He rose, raising his wiry arms in gesture as he spoke. "Think of all the opportunities available through television and the Internet. There's no telling how far we could go! I look at all these young black pastors out here filling up arenas and letting God use them to reach the masses. There's no reason we can't make that kind of impact too. With your guidance and wisdom, I can lead this church to heights most people never even thought possible."

Jeremiah took stock of Eldon's enthusiasm. "Wow, I've never heard you talk like this before. I thought I was going to have to sell you on the idea of taking over the reins, but it looks like you've already put some thought into it, Minister."

"I have. This is the vision God has given me for this church. Don't get me wrong, though. You have my absolute loyalty," affirmed Eldon. "I hope you never question my commitment to this church and seeing it grow to its full potential. I know that there's so much more that God wants us to do here."

"I don't question your commitment to this church. I just hope your commitment to my daughter will be that strong."

"Oh, it is," Eldon covered quickly, sitting back down, a little deflated. "It will be. That goes without saying."

"As a father, I need to hear you say it," Jeremiah added gravely, peering at Eldon over his glasses through large, dark eyes.

Eldon sat upright and looked Jeremiah squarely in the eyes. "You have my word. If Catt does me the honor of giving me her hand in marriage, she'll never want for anything a day in her life. I'll love her until the Lord calls me home and, if He lets me, I'll love her for all eternity in heaven."

Jeremiah chuckled. "All right, don't overdo it. I believe you."

Eldon exhaled, relieved. "I really care for your daughter, sir. I'd do anything to make her happy."

"That's what every father wants to hear, son. And re-member—I said I was *thinking* about retiring. I haven't booked my plane ticket to Florida just yet!"

Eldon began stammering, attempting to apologize again for being overzealous. Jeremiah held up his hand to stop him. "Don't apologize for being eager to do God's work. Just make sure you're motivated by—"

He was interrupted by his receptionist buzzing into the office. "Pastor, the contractor is here," she announced. "He wants to go over the plans for the choir room reno-vations if you have a minute."

"Yes, I'll be right out," Jeremiah spoke into the re-ceiver and stood up. "You wait here, Minister. This'll only take a minute. I want to finish our conversation."

Once the pastor departed, Eldon seized the oppor-tunity to take stock of the office and what could soon be his new digs. The mahogany furnishings, shiny plaques, and relics from Jeremiah's extensive travel made Eldon's modest office pale in comparison.

"Not that I'm complaining, of course," he mumbled, skimming over a framed letter to Jeremiah from the mayor thanking him for the work he had done in the community. "But the Lord wouldn't have sent me here, where I'm clearly needed, if all He wanted me to do is stay in the background."

Eldon moseyed over to Jeremiah's office bathroom and studied his profile in the mirror, admiring his bas-ketball player physique. He even looked like a pastor, or at least the way he thought a pastor should look—distinguished, debonair, and handsome. He adjusted his dark-framed glasses and smoothed his hand over his neatly trimmed goatee. There was no denying that the Lord had blessed him with good genes. While he honestly felt Jeremiah was a man of God, the graying portly pastor was not the image Faith Temple needed to project in order to attract the young, upwardly mobile crowd the church needed in order to stay viable.

Eldon's office tour led him to the pastor's vacated chair. The taut but smooth leather all but invited him to sit down. He stared at the leather recliner, thinking of all the power that came along with it: power to change lives, to make things happen with the stroke of a pen, and to lead a congregation like a fearless shepherd leading his flock.

Besides, wasn't he just as smart as Jeremiah? Just as charismatic? Just as anointed? Plus, he had youth and energy on his side. Who better than he to lead the church? Jeremiah had given his word that it would happen sooner or later. Of course, *sooner* was always better than *later*.

Unable to resist the urge any longer, Eldon eased down in the chair, letting the soft leather envelop his skin.

"One day this will all be mine," he said to himself, settling in rather comfortably. "The chair, the office, the respect—all of it!"

He reclined back, thinking how easily he could get used to this. And all he had to do was bide his time and marry the lovely Catt Cason.

"Yep," he thought aloud, kicking his heels up on Jeremiah's desk and gazing at a picture of Catt. "I could get *real* used to this."

Chapter 3

Catt Cason alternated her right foot between the brake and the accelerator in the midst of Charlotte's downtown morning rush. Thirty-one years of living had brought her to the conclusion that there were three things in life that were inevitable: taxes, death, and traffic. She glanced down at her clock. It was already a quarter until eight, and she was still at least twenty minutes away from work. She hated being late. The only thing that frustrated her more than being late was having to deal with other people being late, which was practically a daily occurrence at the offices of Telegenic, where she'd worked as a formulating chemist for the past five years.

She released an exasperated sigh as she watched another minute roll by on the clock. Then she remembered that she had been praying for God to grant her more patience. She had hoped He would just make her a more patient person, not put her in situations that required her to exercise patience. She adjusted her seat belt. It had gotten snug around her stomach again, burying itself within the creases of excess skin and fat.

"I've got to start back working out," she noted, then looked in the rearview mirror. She fingered her bang a little and smoothed a wayward strand of hair from her face. Her nearly-slanted eyes seemed to shine under the strategically placed gold eye shadow, enhanced by her full fuchsia lips and cappuccino skin. Her heavy form seemed to fit her assertive and take-no-prisoners nature. Chubby or not, she was still a woman who knew when and how to get what she wanted and look fabulous while doing so.

When she finally dashed into the building at 8:10, the lobby looked exactly as it did every morning when she arrived—empty, except the lone janitor, Buck, who politely nodded to her as he pushed his broom across the floor and was always kind enough to brew the coffee.

Catt was always the first in her department to arrive and often the last to leave in the evening. The other staff members usually didn't stumble in until after nine-thirty, largely because the company execs wanted to keep them happy. As long as the highly efficient chemists continued to churn out top-notch products, no one minded overlooking a late morning or an extended lunch break. Usually by the time her colleagues came dragging in, scrounging for a cup of coffee and a quick pick-me-up, Catt would have slipped in a morning prayer, a little Bible study, and have gotten through a third of the items on her to-do list.

Catt rode the elevator down to the lab and the recently vacated office across from hers, where the former head of Research and Development worked. As always, she braced for the familiar rush of cold air beating across her face when she reached her floor. She switched on the light and made her way past the lab stations and beakers to unlock the door to her office. Then she sat down at her desk. As she was checking her e-mail, Catt was startled by a sound that she wasn't expecting to hear: another person.

"Who's there?" she called sternly, skittishly gripping the small can of mace suspended from her key chain.

"It's just me," answered Oni Marshall, the company's director of Product Development.

Catt relaxed. "You're off to an early start!" she noted as Oni scudded past her office in a black pencil skirt and high-heeled boots. The added inches gave her nearly six-foot frame even more of a commanding presence. "Maybe we can convince these other slackers to do the same."

"Whoa, don't take me off the *slacker* list just yet," cautioned Oni. Oni's tardiness was usually on account of her insatiable sexual appetite that had been temporarily quenched the night before. She pulled out a compact and started fiddling with her pixie cut hair in the mirror. "I'm only here because the new R&D starts today. I want to show him around and let him get a feel for the company before everyone gets here."

"What's his name again?"

Oni helped herself to a cup of Catt's pot of coffee before answering the question. "His name is Jamal Ford. I still can't believe we lured him away from Mystique Cosmetics. The work he's done for them has been incredible. Since he started there a few years ago, their sales have nearly doubled. He's a genius in the lab."

"Sounds like getting him was a major coup. Have you met him?"

"Only over the phone," replied Oni, taking a sip of coffee. "But from what I hear from the grapevine, brotherman is six feet and three inches of sexy!" Oni crowed with a shiver.

"Are you sure that you didn't hire him for the chemistry he could stir up with you?" quipped Catt.

"Don't worry," Oni assured her. "The shot-callers upstairs have checked out all of his references and credentials; he comes highly recommended. But I wouldn't mind *personally* checking out every single inch of Mr. Ford." Oni grinned mischievously and dashed out.

Catt wasn't convinced that Oni's rationale for hiring this Jamal person was based on logic as much as it was Oni's overactive libido. She decided to do a little research about him on her own. The last thing that they needed was another brainless head of Research and Development for Oni to seduce.

Catt began conducting a search for Jamal Ford on the company's database. Before she could pull anything up, she was distracted by an intoxicating whiff of cologne.

"Today must be my lucky day," touted a deep voice over her shoulder. Catt gasped and whirred around. "I knew you had a great voice on the phone, but I had no idea you'd be this beautiful in person." He smiled and extended his hand. "I'm Jamal Ford, and you must be Oni Marshall."

Before Catt could respond with anything other than a return handshake, Jamal peeled off his suit jacket and loosened his tie. "All right, I'm ready to start when you are. Let's get down to business, shall we?"

"I don't think I'm the one you're looking for."

He looked puzzled. "I am in the right place, aren't I?"

"Right place, wrong face. I'm not Oni; I'm Catt. Oni's upstairs in her office. She's expecting you, though."

"Word travels fast around here, doesn't it?" He leaned into her computer and spotted his name on her search engine. "So, what do you do around here other than background checks?" he joked.

Embarrassed that she'd been caught red-handed, Catt clicked off the monitor. "I'm a chemist for the new women's line, and up until last week, I was the lead chemist for our teen cosmetic line."

"Teen line, huh? Sounds fun."

"Fun?" she sneered. "Just because the line targets teens doesn't mean it isn't a lot work, Mr. Ford."

"I didn't say it did. Don't be so defensive."

"Don't be so presumptuous," she snapped.

There was an awkward silence between them, which Jamal broke by clearing his throat. "I'm guessing you're not a morning person, huh?" he added.

She rolled her eyes and stirred cream into her coffee. She didn't care how cute he was. It was too early in the morning to be either clever or charming or to tolerate anyone's stab at it.

"So, what did you say your name was again?"

"Catt," she uttered. Hadn't she just told him her name two minutes ago? Catt assumed he was probably the type who had a lot of women's names he had to remember.

Jamal sat down. "I once dated a Catt. She was a hellcat too. Of course, by the time I was through with her, that hellcat had become a sweet little pussycat. She just needed to be tamed, you know what I'm sayin'?" He winked and grinned at her.

Catt crossed her arms in front of her and pierced him with an icy gaze. "*Tamed?* Women aren't dogs, Mr. Ford, or cats, for that matter."

He smirked. "I've known a few who were both."

"Then I guess you should watch the company you keep. You know—birds of a feather and whatnot," she added sweetly.

Jamal took the hint and turned off the charm, easing back into business mode. "Well, could you go tell Miss Marshall I'm here?"

Before Catt could tell Jamal exactly where *he* could go, Oni breezed in with two cups of coffee and a coy smile. "I see the rumors are true," she teased and handed him a cup. "The pictures I've seen online really don't do you justice, Mr. Ford." Jamal blushed and Catt rolled her eyes, facing her computer again. "I see you've met Miss

Catt Cason. She's definitely on the fast track to being one of our top chemists around here. I anticipate the two of you working together rather closely, especially now that we're moving her up from the teens' to our women's line."

"She was just filling me in on how hard she works around here," added Jamal and made a face. "Maybe she works a little *too* hard . . ."

Catt glared in his direction.

Oni stepped in to diffuse the obvious tension. "Why don't you come with me and let me give you the grand tour, Mr. Ford. Then we'll come back and let you two finish getting acquainted. After all, with both of your offices being down here in the lab, the two of you are going to be spending a lot of time together."

Jamal accepted the tour offer, and the two of them jaunted off together.

"And good riddance!" muttered Catt after them. It was rare that she took an instant disliking to someone, but there was something about Mr. Jamal Ford that unsettled her spirit. Maybe it was the way he strutted about like he owned the place or the arrogant aura about him. Nothing good could come from a man like that.

Just as Catt had gotten acclimated to her peaceful surroundings again, Jamal and his cocky smile blazed through the door.

"That Oni is something else!" he remarked, more to himself than to her.

"Well, she's our boss," replied Catt from behind a test tube. "That's all that matters."

"She's a trip. I like her already."

"As a businesswoman and professional, I'm sure she'd rather have your respect than your admiration."

"She has it. You know what I like most about her? She's not afraid to chill out and have a little fun. It's a concept you might want to look into."

Catt looked up from her test tube. "What's *that* supposed to mean?"

"It means maybe the Catt needs to be stroked a little to put a smile on your face instead of that evil frown."

The implication wasn't lost on Catt, and it was the third time that day that he had managed to rile her. She decided right then that it was also going to be the last. "You know—this is *not* going to work!" she stated, setting the test tube back in its place.

"What isn't?"

"My working with you. You are egregious and unprofessional, and I don't think that you're a good fit for this company. In fact, I intend to talk to Oni about it right now." She gathered her things.

"Talk to Oni about what?"

"Let's put it this way—I wouldn't start getting too comfortable around here if I were you."

He seemed both amused and annoyed. "Then it's a good thing you're not me, isn't it?"

"Do you even *know* who I am?" she asked, raising her voice an octave. "I could have you fired *just like that!*" She snapped her fingers to illustrate.

"On what grounds?"

"On the grounds that I refuse to work with you! It's going to be either you or me, and, believe me, Oni is not going to let me walk. I've been here too long and have contributed too much to this company."

"Catt, Telegenic paid big bucks to buy me out of my contract. They're about to launch this new line, and they need my help. I'm at the top of my game, sweetheart," he boasted. "I don't think that they're going to be in a big hurry to fire me because you can't take a joke. Or maybe it's the fact that what I said is true that's got you all beside yourself."

She huffed and marched out. "Oni," she screeched, making a beeline straight to her office. "We need to talk *right now!*"

Chapter 4

For once, Catt was dreading the elevator trip down to the lab, not so much because Jamal would be working there, but because she would have to tread in with her tail between her legs following her diatribe with Jamal and her pointless attempt to get him axed from the company. Perhaps fate would be kind and let Jamal forget that she had threatened to have him fired.

"I heard you talked to Oni. Do I still have a job, or should I start packing?" asked Jamal the moment she stepped off of the elevator. Apparently, fate was a cruel and heartless bastard.

"You're safe," she replied coolly, walking across the tile to her office.

Jamal followed her. "What did you tell her?"

She donned her lab coat and turned on the computer. "I voiced my concerns, but I also added that I'm willing to give you another shot, provided that you're willing to put forth the effort of being a team player. After all, I am a professional, and I realize that certain allowances must be made for the good of the company."

He leaned against the door frame with his arms crossed in front of him and a smirk on his face. "Basically, what you're trying to say is that Oni told you what you could do with all your threats to quit and have me fired."

Her face contorted into a snarl. "Don't push it, Ford," she warned him. "Fear not, though—I fully expect for you to live up to my lowest expectations. You'll dig your own grave without my having to tell Oni anything."

"My work will speak for itself. It always does."

"Well, let's hope so." She skimmed through her e-mails. "Speaking of work, we need to come up with some sort of schedule or arrangement. I think it's better for everyone if we work together as little as possible, don't you agree?"

"No, I don't." He stepped inside of her office. "Oni told me all about you. You're bullheaded but more than that, you're smart and an asset to this company. I need you."

She mocked him. "So, the great and powerful Jamal Ford is admitting that he needs my help?"

"I'm admitting that we could make one heck of a team if you'd let it happen. I know that we got off on the wrong foot, and I apologize for my part in that, but we're stuck together now. How about we just start over; pretend the last hour or so never happened. The last thing I want to do is sabotage our working relationship before it even gets started."

She was stunned. "That's mighty big of you. I appreciate it."

"In that case," he cleared his throat and stood upright, extending his right hand with a conciliatory grin, "I'm Jamal Ford, the new R&D chemist around here. What's your name?"

A reluctant smile crept across her lips. "Catt Cason. Everyone calls me Catt." When she enveloped her hand into his, an electric shock circulated from his hand through her entire body, sending enough heat to warm the Arctic. She quickly snatched her hand back. The exchange didn't appear to have affected him the same way.

They walked out into the lab. Jamal rubbed his hands together in anticipation. "So, Miss Catt Cason, show me what you've got. Let's see what you've been working on."

Catt reached over to her test tubes and pulled out one of the samples. "This is a combination I've been toying with. It's sort of strong yet soft. It's for the woman who wants to run with the big boys but can still pull off femininity and grace."

Jamal inhaled the swab and shook his head. "No, too strong—try again."

"You didn't like that, huh?" She was a little miffed. Not one to be deterred that easily, she handed him another sample. "Okay, how about this one? It's my personal favorite. I think it's perfect for a young woman, maybe a college student, who's into natural, clean scents. What do you think?"

Jamal smelled it and thought for a moment. "Nope; too light."

Catt suppressed her annoyance and passed him a third fragrance. "Maybe the third time will be the charm," she replied through clenched teeth.

After sniffing it, Jamal closed his eyes and shook his head again.

Catt rolled her eyes, fuming. "You said that the last one was too light; the first one was too strong. Can't you make up your mind? What's the problem now?"

"Catt, you're a woman . . . I'm assuming. Would you wear this, let alone *buy* it?"

"I don't see anything wrong with it, just like I didn't see anything wrong with the last two fragrances you rejected."

"That's because you're used to creating products for the teen and young adult lines. This new clientele you're aiming for is very sophisticated and has more discerning tastes. They're not about to plunk down fifty dollars on something that smells like mouthwash. You're in the big leagues now, Catt; no more of that bubble gum stuff."

"I'll have you to know that Ingénue was the number-one fragrance for six months and was our biggest seller last year," she hurled. "*I* was the mastermind behind that."

"Stop being so sensitive. This isn't about you, it's about expanding and creating a better product."

"*Derrick* never had a problem with my work," she uttered in reference to the former R&D head.

"And where is he now? Standing in line at the unemployment office. Overall sales plummeted under his watch, which is why they recruited me. I'm determined to put Telegenic back on top, and I need for you to stop fighting me on this."

"And I need you to stop being a tyrant. That's *not* the way we do things around here."

"Maybe it *should* be. Doing things the old way has cost this company millions."

"Look, Jamal, I know that you think the cosmetic sun rises and falls on you, but the reality is, I don't know anything about you. I don't trust you, and until Oni, who is my *real* boss, directs me to do otherwise, I'll keep doing what I know works, thank you very much!"

Jamal eyed her with disapproval. "You know, I honestly thought that we had settled all of this animosity and attitude." Catt smacked her lips. "Yeah, that's real mature, Catt. Now I understand why they put you in charge of the teen line."

Catt immediately took offense. "I take my job very seriously, and I'm good at what I do. I don't appreciate you stomping in here out of nowhere and crapping all over my hard work!"

"What, so I'm supposed to be impressed because you're good at your job?" he fired back. "You're *supposed* to be good; otherwise, they don't need you. I'm not here to coddle you. This is a business, Catt. People's lives and livelihoods are dependent on this company being a success, and that can't happen if I let you turn out subpar products to keep from hurting your feelings. If you have a problem with me or my way of doing things, you don't have to work. There are plenty of people willing to do what you aren't for the same salary."

"You didn't let me—"

"This conversation is over, Cason. Now get back to work and get it right this time," he ordered and charged into his office, slamming the door behind him.

All of a sudden, Catt was back in third grade getting yelled at by her teacher for spilling glue all over her desk. As she did then, she masked a stern face but was a blubbering mess inside. Catt stopped a tear before it had a chance to escape down her cheek. Then she heard his door creak open a minute later.

"Sorry," he said in a huff. "I shouldn't have yelled at you like that."

She sniffed. "I'm a big girl inside and out, and my skin is a lot thicker than you seem to think it is."

"That's good. You need a tough hide in this business." He emerged from his office and placed a hand on her shoulder. "Besides, I wouldn't want to upset you."

She snatched away from him. "You didn't, okay? Now, if you don't mind, I have work to do."

He turned her toward him. "Why don't we work on it together?"

"I've got it," she insisted. "I don't need your help."

"You need my help, and then some. This is never going to work if you can't learn to give up some control and trust that you're not the only one around here who knows what they're doing."

She brushed off his comment with a brusque, "I just can't figure out for the life of me why God and Oni saddled me with you."

"Maybe I'm that thorn in your flesh that's supposed to keep you on your knees," he replied good-naturedly. "Or maybe I was sent here by the Lord to drive you crazy and, ultimately, turn you into a better person."

"God sends us good and perfect gifts," she retorted.

"He sends you what you need, even if you don't know you need it yet."

"Oh, so you're a prophet too?" she asked flippantly.

"Hardly. You're doing good if you catch me in church most Sundays, but I am a chemist, and I know another good chemist when I see one. And you're good, Catt." He moved in a little closer and lowered his voice. "But that doesn't mean I can't make you better."

Catt backed up. Having him so close made her inexplicably nervous. "You're very arrogant. Has anyone ever told you that?"

"All the time," he admitted. "But eventually they come around." He began toying with some of the other fragrances that Catt had been working on.

"Those aren't ready to be scrutinized yet," she told him. "They're still in the developing stage."

"Kind of like the two of us," he mused. Jamal inhaled one of her samples. "This fragrance is a lot like you . . . bold, sassy . . . complicated."

"Does this mean you like it?"

He returned the sample to its socket. His eyes washed over her body. "Let's just say that the data is inconclusive," said Jamal and walked out of the door, still as much an enigma to Catt as ever.

Chapter 5

At the end of her long work day, Catt sought the comfort at the bottom of a quart of triple-fudge brownie ice cream and a rerun of *Oprah*. As Oprah's expert de jour was expounding on the dangers of emotional eating, the doorbell rang.

"When did you get back?" asked Catt when she found her best friend and hairstylist, Toria Turner, on her door step.

"Are you going to let me in or not? It's hot out here!" she exclaimed, lifting her thick mass of braids to get some air underneath.

Catt crossed her arms and frowned. "I don't know. You look a little empty-handed."

"Don't worry." Toria pushed her way into Catt's living room. "Mama sent you her sweet potato pie just like she promised. It's at home." Toria slouched into the sofa, making herself comfortable as usual. "So what have I been missing around here?"

"A lot." Catt sat down beside her. "And take your feet off my coffee table."

Toria smacked her teeth and begrudgingly complied. "Can't too much happen in a week," she deadpanned in her deep, Southern drawl.

"Maybe not in your world but in mine, a week can hold a lifetime of drama."

Toria exhaled. "All right, who or what has Oni done— or *not* done—now?"

"This doesn't have anything to do with her directly. It's about this new R&D they burdened me with."

Toria absently twisted her braids into a thick rope. "What's the problem?"

"The problem is that he's arrogant and—"

Toria stopped. "Oh, it's a *he?*" she asked, intrigued.

"There are a few other things I can call him if you'd like! I can't stand the way he flaunts about all self-righteous with his fancy suits and smooth tongue and worms his way into everyone's good graces, especially Oni's. I don't know why I'm the only who sees through this guy."

Toria picked up a copy of *Essence* lying on Catt's coffee table. "Is he incompetent?"

"No, not really," admitted Catt. "I mean, I've seen better, but he knows his stuff."

"Has he been giving you a hard time?"

"Not in any obvious way but . . . I can't describe it, Tori. It's all very covert and indirect."

Toria looked up from the magazine. "Okay, so, what exactly is it about him that you don't like?"

Catt was stuck. "I don't know. There's no *one* glaring thing. It's lots of little things."

Toria snickered. "It sounds to me like you might have a thing for him."

Catt was aghast. "*What?* I just told you that I can't stand him. How could you possibly think that based on what I just said?"

Toria directed her hands toward Catt. "Look at you— you're all worked up over this guy. The only time you get like that is when you really like somebody."

"Toria, I think you were out in that sun too long down in Miami." Catt got up and disappeared into the kitchen.

"So, what are you going to do about what's his name—the chemist?" asked Toria loud enough for Catt to hear her.

Catt returned with two sodas. "Who, Jamal?" She passed a soda to Toria and popped the can on hers. "I don't know. Obviously, getting him fired isn't the answer. I already tried that. I'm just going to sit back and wait for him to hang himself. He can't go on fooling everyone forever."

Toria took a swig from her can. "Why are you so down on the brother? Maybe this dude really is what he says he is."

Catt shook her head. "I'm not letting my guard down for a minute. I have a bad feeling about him, and my instincts are never wrong about this stuff. I don't trust him. Believe me when I tell you, girl, Jamal Ford is trouble with a capital T!"

Chapter 6

For once, Catt didn't indulge in her first cup of coffee in the solitude of her office. Instead, she opted to have it in the lobby of the building where everyone else usually gathered for office gossip and idle conversation before putting in a day's work. She made this decision partially to avoid being alone in the lab with Jamal but mostly to find out what other people were saying about him. She wasn't surprised to discover that most of the women in the office were already fawning over the charming new chemist.

"I met your new partner," mentioned Francine Tukes, one of the quality control chemists, as they huddled around the percolator. "It must be nice to be stuck in isolation with him all day."

Catt played it cool, not wanting to appear overly interested or too religious to notice when an attractive man had entered their midst. "He's all right if you go for that conceited, Boris Kodjoe-wannabe type."

Francine eyed Catt incredulously. "Who doesn't?"

"You must be talking about that oh-so-delicious Jamal Ford," butt in the receptionist Michelle, from her desk. "He's so charming and sexy."

Catt noticed that Michelle's blouse was cut lower than usual, presumably to give Jamal an eyeful as soon as he walked into the building. "He's seems a little arrogant to me," admitted Catt.

Francine appeared puzzled. "Everyone else says he's so nice. I know I didn't get that vibe from him when I met him." She sipped her coffee. "Then again, I was only with him for about twenty seconds. You're with him all day, so I guess you would know."

"What's it like working with him, Catt?" asked Michelle, who was practically salivating.

"Yeah, Catt, tell us what it's like working with him," echoed a voice from behind. It was Jamal. Catt froze. "Good morning, ladies."

Michelle cleared her throat and sat upright, embarrassed by Jamal overhearing them. "Good morning, Mr. Ford."

"Good morning, Miss Billings," he replied graciously. "Good morning to you too, Miss Tukes."

Francine glowed. "You remembered my name. How are you doing this fine day?"

Jamal punched in their floor on the elevator dial. "Great. I'm looking forward to another productive day here at Telegenic." He nodded to Catt. "What's up, Catt?"

"Hello, Jamal." They exchanged awkward, tense glances. The elevator finally opened up and invited him in. "Well, you beautiful women have a good day, and, Catt, I guess I'll see you in the lab."

"I guess you will," said Catt a little testily. It stung a bit that he was able to readily recall Michelle's and Francine's names but had forgotten hers two minutes after they met the day before.

"He is just as fine as he wants to be," uttered Francine as the elevator door closed in on him.

Michelle readjusted her blouse to make it appear more conservative. "You ain't the only one who thinks so. The secretary over at Mystique said he used to have women calling up there left and right."

"Oh?" replied Catt.

Francine wasn't shocked. "You know a man like that keeps women."

The statement hit a nerve with Catt. "I just hope he keeps them out of my lab. We have enough to worry about without adding loose women to the list."

Having had her fill of coffee and tidbits about Jamal, Catt hopped on the next available elevator and braced herself for the rush of air and for the latest round of clashing with her new lab partner.

The clash that she'd been gearing up for never came. As soon as Catt entered the lab, Jamal brushed past her with a stack of folders bundled under his arm. He uttered a barely audible "The lab is all yours" before being absorbed by the elevator.

Meetings and other obligations kept Catt from seeing him for the rest of the morning. She enjoyed having the lab to herself again, but the smell of his cologne lingered long after he left, much like his presence.

By the time lunch rolled around, Jamal still hadn't returned. Catt was so engrossed in her work that she'd practically forgotten he existed or that she had promised to meet her father for lunch. Noting the time, she quickly put away her test tubes and made a mad dash to McCormick and Schmick's Seafood Restaurant to meet Jeremiah.

"Sorry I'm late, Daddy," apologized Catt as she scurried into the restaurant twenty minutes late. She kissed her father on the cheek. "I got held up at work."

"I've told you about working so hard," he warned her as he stood up to pull out Catt's chair for her.

"You don't have to remind me," she sang and sat down.

The waiter came over to their table and placed menus down in front of them. "Is your entire party here now, sir?"

"Yes," answered Catt. "He was waiting on me."

"Umm, there's actually one more who'll be joining us," said Jeremiah.

Catt blinked. *"One more?"*

"I'll give you a few more minutes," said the waiter before speeding off.

"Who else is coming?" asked Catt.

"Someone from the church," he answered quickly. "So tell me what's going on in the cosmetic world? Y'all still in a panic over there about sales?"

"Something like that," divulged Catt.

"I've been praying for you. It's kind of tough on everyone with this economy."

"Yeah, we've hit a slump, but we'll bounce back. We always do. Oni just hired this new wonder boy who they think is the answer to all of our problems."

"I take it you're not sold on the new guy."

Catt's expression changed. "Daddy, there's just something off about him. My spirit gets very restless whenever he's around me."

"Have you prayed about it; asked God to give you some discernment about this person?"

"Not yet," reported Catt. "Everybody seems to think that I'm the problem and that he's such a great guy. I'm trying to keep an open mind, but there's still this negative feeling about him that I can't shake."

"Just pray. Ask God to bind any demonic force at work that may be hindering you from working together. Turn it over to the Lord. I guarantee you'll get better results than trying to figure this thing out by yourself."

"You're right," she conceded. "God can certainly handle the situation and Jamal a lot better than I can."

"You would do well to listen to your old dad," advised Jeremiah. "I've gotten pretty good at knowing what's best for my little girl. Speaking of which . . ." Jeremiah waved to get Eldon's attention and called, "Minister, over here."

Eldon crisscrossed his way through the maze of tables to get to theirs. He shook Jeremiah's hand and caressed Catt's. "How are you doing today, Sister Cason?"

Catt plastered on a smile. "I'm great. I didn't know you'd be joining us."

"It's not a problem, is it?" asked Eldon before sitting down.

Catt shook her head. "Of course not, just wasn't expecting you, that's all."

"My being here is a pleasant surprise, I hope."

Catt didn't reply but smiled politely.

Eldon picked up a menu. "So, what are you two having?"

Catt skimmed the menu. "Just a Cobb salad for me. I'm trying to watch my figure these days."

Eldon gave her the once-over. "I don't know why. I think you're perfect the way you are."

She doubted that. "Thank you, Eldon, but it's more about being healthy than it is about trying to squeeze into a size two."

"The minister exercises quite often," said Jeremiah. "Maybe the two of you ought to work out together."

"I would love that," Eldon chimed in. "Working out is always more productive when you have a partner. Everything is."

Catt caught the hint. "I'll keep that in mind, Eldon."

"Sweetheart, you ought to see some of the exciting things the minister is coming up with for our youth," suggested Jeremiah after their orders had been taken and their plates brought out.

"I love kids. It's truly a labor of love," said Eldon.

"You definitely have a calling for it," acknowledged Catt. "I've seen the way you are with the children and the teens. You're going to make a great dad."

"I'm sure he will. A great husband too," declared Jeremiah, cracking open his snow crabs.

Catt cut her eyes at her father. Could he be more obvious?

Eldon hung his head bashfully. "Your father is very generous with the kind words."

"My father is a lot of things," mumbled Catt before sipping her tea.

"All right, what can I say?" confessed Jeremiah, exasperated. "I think you two would make a fine couple."

Catt shook her head. This was not the first, and probably not the last, time that Jeremiah had taken it upon himself to find her a suitable mate. "If you don't mind, Daddy, I prefer to leave the matchmaking to my Heavenly Father, not my earthly one."

Her father objected. "Sometimes the Lord works through others, you know that, Catt."

"And sometimes we get in the Lord's way when we try to force things to happen, don't we, Daddy?" countered Catt. The irritation was now detectable in her voice. "God said, 'I know *my* plans for you.' He never said anything about needing us to help out with our own agendas."

Jeremiah put down his fork and wiped his hands. "Uh-huh," he grunted and rose from his chair. "If you two will excuse me, I need to make a phone call."

Catt sighed as she watched her father walk away. "I'm sorry you got caught in the middle of all this, Eldon. My father is on a mission to get me down the aisle by any means—and *minister*—necessary!"

Eldon laughed. "His heart is in the right place."

"Yeah, but his nose isn't!"

Eldon leaned forward. "Truth be told, Catt, I didn't need him to sell me on the idea of you being a good catch. I concluded that on my own a long time ago."

She smiled. "I think you're a good man, Eldon. I hope that we can grow to become great friends."

He sat back in his chair. "So all you're looking for is friendship, huh?"

Catt shrugged. "I don't really think about much else. Work ties up a lot of my time. Plus, I have my ministries at the church to worry about. There's not really a lot of room in my life for much else."

Eldon began eating again. "Church and work—that's really it for you?"

"Well, I like sports, and I love to read too," she added, pushing her salad around her plate. She wondered if her life was really as boring as it sounded.

"Anything other than the Bible?" Eldon asked.

"Sure. I like poetry."

Eldon lit up. "I do too." He was grateful to see that they had something other than the Lord and ambition in common. "Who's your favorite poet?"

She mulled it over. "Wow, there are so many, but I have to say Sonia Sanchez and Stephany immediately come to mind."

"Who's Stephany? I've never heard of her."

"She's kind of an unknown. I started getting into her stuff in undergrad. She's one of those poets who started building a name for herself during the '60s."

Eldon drew a blank. "The name's not ringing a bell. Do you know anything of hers by heart? I might recognize some of her work if I hear it."

"*In the silence of the city night when the lonely watch the sky in yearning, I at rest beside you, lie in peace. I searched a thousand skies before you came,*" recited Catt.

"Is that hers?"

"Yes, isn't it beautiful?" she sighed.

"It probably would be if I knew what the heck she was talking about."

"She's talking about a woman who goes her whole life searching for love, and she finally finds him. Then she looks around at all of the lonely people in the world, and she realizes how blessed she is to have true love. She doesn't have to watch the sky or roam or be alone anymore."

"Is that what you're doing—watching the sky, roaming, looking for love?" posed Eldon.

"I guess we all are in a way. I just hope I find love the same time it finds me, you know?"

Eldon nodded. "Believe me, I've done my fair share of looking. But who knows." He reached across the table and lifted her chin. "Maybe the one I've been searching for all of my life has been right here in front of me all along."

Chapter 7

The next few weeks of working with Jamal mirrored the day he rushed by her to catch the elevator. Their interactions consisted mostly of seeing each other in spurts as he raced from one meeting to another with Oni or some other executive within the company. His name was barely even mentioned in office gossip anymore as most of the women at Telegenic had concluded that either he was all business or was sleeping with Oni.

"Where's your shadow?" asked Catt, looking up from her test tube. "You and Oni have been joined at the hip lately."

"We've been collaborating with the other departments trying to finalize everything for the meeting tomorrow. You do intend to be there, don't you?"

"Oni's memo didn't give me the impression that it was optional."

"It's not, but I really want you there. With so much going on and so many changes being made, we need your input."

Catt threw him a side-eyed glance accompanied by a sarcastic, "Yeah, right."

"Pardon?"

"You don't want my opinion, Jamal. If that were the case, perhaps I would have been included in some of these secret strategy sessions with you and Oni. No, you just want me to smile, say yes, and do as I'm told like some kind of mindless waif."

He frowned. "Why do you always act like there's some kind of conspiracy going on? Respect the chain of command like everyone else." He swiped the test tube away from her.

"Hey!" She snatched it back.

Jamal retrieved it again. "I want to see what you've been working on. Gotta make sure you haven't been slackin' off in my absence."

"Slacking off? In case you haven't noticed, I've been chained to this lab for the past two weeks."

He took a whiff of the product. "Did you create this by yourself?"

"It's just something I've been playing around with. I'm not asking for a critique yet," clarified Catt in an attempt to squash his latest round of rejections before he fired them off.

Jamal smelled it again. "Is it for the men's line?"

"It could be. I think it's too rugged for women." She revealed the truth. "Actually, my dad's birthday is coming up, and I thought it would be nice to give him his own signature fragrance. Don't worry—I haven't been wasting company time working on this. I do it before or after work."

"I'm not as worried about you wasting the company's time as I am you wasting company resources," he grumbled. "But I like it. I want Oni to take a look at it."

She beamed with pride. "So I've finally created something you like?"

"Two things, actually. I've been doing a little work on one of the fragrances you started on that I thought you had some potential. Here, check this out."

She inhaled the invigorating scent. "I love it. It's clean, not too flowery or overwhelming." She sniffed it again. "Very feminine."

"Let's try a little bit on you." He dabbed a few drops on her wrists. "How's that?"

She stretched out her arm to him. "You smell it, and tell me what you think."

He took her hand and lifted her wrist to his nose. "It's sexy and seductive." He flashed her a smile. "Or maybe it just smells that way on you." He daubed some on her neck and leaned into it. "I especially like it right here."

Catt's head was starting to swoon with his being so close to her. "Maybe we should call Oni and tell her the good news," she suggested in a futile effort to distract him or herself.

He wrapped his arms around her waist and pulled her to him, burying his face in her neck.

She was taken unawares, paralyzed into submission. "Jamal, what are you doing?" she squalled.

He lifted his head. "Research."

"Research?"

"Yeah, this is how I conduct my analysis."

Catt pushed him away. "Your methods are very unconventional . . . and extremely inappropriate!"

"Don't get your dandruff up. It's not anything personal. I'm just trying to determine how this fragrance affects men when it is worn by a beautiful woman."

She was still flushed. It was undeniable: Jamal Ford *definitely* had a way with women. "And what was your conclusion, Mr. Ford?"

He arrested her with his gaze. "Once again, the data was inconclusive."

Catt composed herself and slipped a lock of hair behind her ear. "For future reference, please don't mistake me for one of these lovesick women throwing themselves at you around here. Your charm is wasted on me."

Jamal jotted something down on his clipboard and laughed a little. "Whatever, Catt . . . you know you liked it."

Catt rolled her eyes. "You're so smug. It's infuriating."

He turned and addressed her head-on. "Not smug, just sure of myself."

"I believe the phrase you're looking for is *full* of yourself."

"But that's what you love about me, isn't it?" asked Jamal with a wink.

"Try *loathe* about you."

"You know what I love about you?" he went on. "I like it when you squint your eyes and your lips get all pouty like that. It's kind of sexy."

She could feel heat rising to her face. "I don't think this conversation is appropriate for the workplace. Besides, I'm a Christian. I don't like engaging in conversations and acts that compromise or contradict my faith."

"Chill out, Catt. It was a joke." Turning his back to her, Jamal began shuffling papers attached to his clipboard. "Dang, don't they do that where you come from?"

Catt put her hands on her hips and looked at him squarely in the face. "Why do you do that?"

"Do what?"

"I mean, one minute, you're acting like my drill sergeant and the next . . ."

He set the clipboard down. "The next what?"

"I don't know. It's like you're messing with my head or something," she blurted out. "Just forget it," she huffed.

"I believe the word you're looking for is *flirting*," filled in Jamal. "Does it bother you—the flirting, I mean? Do you like it?" He pressed against her. "Do you want me to stop?"

Her head started spinning again. "Jamal, we can't . . ."

"Can't what . . . this?" He leaned down and set his lips above hers as if he were going to kiss her. Fumes from an overheated beaker caught his attention, and he immediately broke away from Catt to attend to the overflowing beaker behind them.

A thin cloud of smoke hovered above him. He smiled back at Catt. "You see what you do to me? That was a close one," he said, pouring the scorched mixture down the drain.

In more ways than one, thought Catt.

She wondered if he was just joking around again or if he was really going to kiss her. "Now you see why I don't approve of all this playing around in the lab."

"I was just trying to get you to loosen up. You're wound way too tight. This is an office, not a military base. Even Christians are allowed to have some fun every now and then."

She didn't really like that he thought she was a prude nor did she like the emotions he managed to stir up inside of her when he looked at her the way he was right then. "It's getting late. Maybe we should call it a day."

"Are you sure? Things were just starting to heat up." Jamal locked eyes with her and moved to touch her face.

Suddenly a bell chimed, and the elevator slid open.

A leggy, saucy-eyed woman stepped off and strutted past Catt and over to Jamal. "They said I could find you down here." She tossed her long ringlets back and held up a gold watch. "You left this on the nightstand."

"Thanks," he replied warily and clasped it onto his wrist. "I was looking for it this morning."

"I was looking for a lot of things this morning too. You'll never guess where I found my panties." She giggled and clamped her arms around his neck. "Will I see you again tonight?"

He licked his lips. "I'll call you."

"I'll be waiting." She kissed him and departed.

Jamal approached Catt, who pretended not to pay the whole scene any attention. She silently prayed, asking God to forgive her for the moment of weakness she had with Jamal and thanked Him for bringing back to her remembrance of the kind of operator he really was.

She began readjusting her formula. "Don't!" barked Catt when he tried to assist her.

"I thought that we were working on this together."

"You thought wrong. Excuse me." She swept by him and moved to another station.

"I want to finish our conversation."

"Yeah, well, I want to finish this up so I can go home before dawn." She looked up at him. "You don't have to hover over me. I'm sure you have skirts to chase or something else important like that."

"At least let me apologize for what just happened. Even I have to admit that wasn't very professional. It won't happen again."

"Yes, it will, Jamal, because that's just who you are. You have no respect for the workplace and, obviously, no respect for women. You may be a whiz in the laboratory, but you're a complete dud when it comes to having integrity and character."

"And you're a real killjoy when it comes to anything even closely resembling fun or having a life. Even the Lord Himself took Sundays off!"

"You don't need to speak about things you clearly have no concept of, such as righteous living. If you're going to give in to every lust and temptation that crosses your path, at least have the decency to keep it behind closed doors."

"So you're so holier-than-thou that you never get tempted? Don't you have the same sexual urges as everyone else?"

"The Bible tells us to flee fornication and to resist temptation," she admonished. "You should try it sometime."

"I suppose it's very easy to resist temptation when there's no one out there trying to tempt you. I'm no expert on the subject, but isn't it just as big a sin to have the desire? The only difference between you and me is that I act on it instead of denying it."

"You're not going to make me feel bad for trying to live right."

"Unlike you, I don't judge the way you live your life. I just think you need to get one outside of the church and the lab . . . and the kitchen."

It wasn't anything she hadn't heard before, but that last comment was a kick in the gut. She was quiet a moment to recover. "Say what you want, but I live a life that I'm not ashamed to bring before the Lord. You, on the other hand, seem to live a life that would make the devil blush. Don't think you won't have to account for that on the Day of Judgment."

Jamal conceded. "Well, Catt, I'll make a deal with you. Why don't you keep your Bible-totin', scripture-quotin' observations to yourself, and I'll keep my hedonistic desires to myself. Deal?"

She threw up her hand in capitulation. "Fine."

"And don't think I don't know the truth either," tossed in Jamal. "I saw the way you were looking at me when you thought I was about to kiss you. I wasn't going to, by the way, but it's painfully obvious that you need to be kissed by a real man, very badly, I might add. Of course, we won't even get into what else you need to have a real man do for you. Maybe then you could chill out some."

She made a face and returned to her work. Catt didn't know if she was more bothered by the fact that he'd said it or the fact that there could be some truth to it.

Chapter 8

"He tried to pull rank on me today. Can you believe that?" recounted Catt to Toria over the rush of the water being sprayed down her scalp. "Does he *really* think I'm intimidated by him because he has that little title and a bigger paycheck? *Please!*"

Toria lathered shampoo into Catt's thick mane. "It's been a long time since I've seen a guy get to you like this."

"And talk about attitude!" ranted Catt. "He acts like he's God's gift to Telegenic, like there's no way the company could function without him. What does he think we've been doing for the past five years?"

Toria shrugged. "Waiting for him to show up, I suppose."

"Just to show you how unprofessional he is, he had the nerve to have some hoochie up in there today slobbering all over him, talking about how she couldn't find her panties this morning. And for the record, she wasn't all that cute, and her outfit—can we say—total skank?"

Toria thought for a few seconds. "So how long do you think it'll be?"

"How long before what—he gets fired or gets an STD?" asked Catt.

Toria waited until she finished rinsing Catt's hair again to reply. "No, before you're letting him light your fire in and out of the lab."

"Tori, are you *still* on that? How many times must I tell you that the mere thought of him touching me makes me want to get tested for rabies? And you know what? That son of a gun tried to kiss me! Can you believe that?" exclaimed Catt. "Just out of the blue, right there in the middle of the lab!"

"Were you disappointed that it wasn't successfully executed?"

Catt gagged. "God, no! I have done nothing but try to stay as far away from him as I possibly can. And out of nowhere, he just ups and tries to kiss me, saying I looked like I needed to be kissed. If I do, I certainly don't need to be kissed by him."

Toria laughed. "Did you slap him when he tried?"

Catt hesitated in responding. "Well . . . no," she finally admitted.

"Why not?"

"With someone like Jamal, a slap would have just turned him on even more."

Toria gathered Catt's wet hair in a towel. "Did the almost-kiss turn *you* on?"

"What kind of question is that, Tori? That man repulses me. Why would I want him to kiss me?"

"That's not what I asked you."

There was no way that she could lie to the person who knew her best, but Catt wasn't ready to reveal the truth to herself, much less to anyone else. "I am turned on by kisses from men I actually like," she replied, dodging a direct response.

Toria sat Catt down in an empty styling chair. "You just need to be honest with yourself, Catt. Every single thing he does causes some kind of reaction in you. What else could it mean?"

"It could mean any number of things, but what it *doesn't* mean is that I am in any way attracted to him, especially given the way he runs through women and lives any ol' kind of raggedy life."

Toria began combing out Catt's hair. "You know what they say about that thin line—"

"It's *not* a thin line. More like a large ream of yellow police tape with '*do not cross*' stamped all over it!"

Toria laughed out loud. "Point taken! But he does seem to spark more of an interest for you than the minister."

"You mean Eldon?" Catt smacked her teeth. "Girl, my dad already has us married with three or four buns in the oven, a cat, a white picket fence, *and* a dog!"

"Is that your vision too?"

"I don't know. I mean, Eldon's a good dude and all, but something's missing. He doesn't have that *umph* factor, you know what I'm saying?"

"I know, but too much *umph* can get you into trouble. Need I mention Greg?" asked Toria in reference to Catt's last boyfriend.

"No, you need not! But I will say that Greg could capture and keep my attention. I can't say the same for the minister."

"Can you say the same for Jamal?"

"Jamal is not my type, and I'm almost positive I'm not his. He seems to go more for the beautiful airhead model chicks, and that's not me."

Toria broached her with caution. "So we're back to the weight issue?"

"The weight is not an issue for me. I'm comfortable in my own skin, but for guys like Jamal, it's *the* issue. Do you know he had the nerve to tell me that I need to get a life outside of the kitchen?"

Toria winced. "Ouch!"

Catt shook her head. "I'd never waste my time on a man like that. Plus, our lifestyles are just too different.

Can you imagine what it would be like if I brought him home to meet my father? Daddy would be casting out demons left and right!"

"What are you going to do if he tries to kiss you again?"

"He won't," guaranteed Catt. "I made sure of that."

Toria stopped combing. "But what if he does?"

Catt pursed her lips together, unable to answer.

Chapter 9

Francine bumped into Catt inside the elevator the next morning. "I guess you're headed to the big mystery meeting too, huh?" she asked.

"I think we've all been summoned," replied Catt. "Whatever is going down must be pretty major. Jamal and Oni have been hard at work on it for weeks."

"Well, you know Oni," hinted Francine. "No doubt she's been mixing a little play with all that work."

Catt followed Francine into the conference room, where they were met by Oni, Jamal, and the cadre of cosmetic chemists.

"Is everybody here?" began Oni, rising from her seat at the head of the conference table.

Jamal looked around, then positioned himself at her side. "It looks like everyone is here and accounted for."

"Great, let's get down to business, shall we?" Oni turned to address the group. "As all of you know by now, Telegenic has taken a hit lately. Our sales are down, the competition is killing us, and we're struggling for business during a time when most people are more concerned about putting food on the table than they are about the new lipstick colors we've added for spring.

"Telegenic is in desperate need of a new image and a reason to get our customers excited again, which is why we hired Mr. Ford here. I'm sure by now all of you have had the pleasure of meeting him."

Jamal nodded.

Three of the women responded with flirtatious smiles. Catt rolled her eyes.

"We're in the process of rolling out our new fragrances for fall, but before we officially launch, we would like to get a campaign going to generate a stir. By the time it's released in October, we want these fragrances to fly off the shelf."

"Who's our target?" asked Francine, taking notes.

Jamal spoke up. "Women, of course, professional, thirty-plus."

"Are we going for something fun, something sexy—what?" asked another.

"All of the above. The head honchos are giving us carte blanche on this. All they want is a product that's going to knock the consumers off their feet."

Francine looked up from her note taking. "Do we have a name for it?"

Oni turned to Jamal. "Mr. Ford, do you want to answer this one?"

He cleared his throat and addressed the room. "Oni and I have been working with the marketing department, tossing around ideas for a few days now. We wanted the name to convey passion and sensuality without being overtly sexual. Of course, it had to be something original and something that could draw our buyers to the counter, and that's when we came up with it." He paused, milking the suspense as much as he could. "We want to call this line Allure. The name alone evokes magnetism, sex appeal, intrigue."

Oni jumped in. "And we're going all out here—perfume, makeup, lotion. We're rolling out the fragrances first, which, Catt, you and Jamal will be in charge of. Telegenic wants to have the first of it on the shelves by October, in time for Christmas."

"Is that going to give us enough time for data testing and research?" asked Catt.

"It's going to have to," explained Oni. "Telegenic's sales have taken a dive for the past two quarters. Unless we do something major, the problem is only going to get worse. We've got to get people talking about us again. More important, we've got to get them to the cash register—the sooner, the better. Your department is the heart and soul of this company. We can't afford to fail here."

Jamal spoke again. "In an effort to do some out-of-box promoting, Oni and I have decided to hit all of our major markets from here to New York on a promotional blitz for the new products," he revealed. "Over the next three weeks, we'll be setting up shop in Cleveland, Chicago, Baltimore, New York, Milwaukee, and Memphis, just to name a few. We'll be housed in the cities' major shopping districts giving out samples, surveying the customers, and really getting out there to connect with our buyers. We don't want them to feel like they're buying from a company. We want them to feel like they're shopping with friends, like they've had some input in the products we're putting out there."

"Obviously, this is a massive undertaking, but it's what we feel we have to do to get out of the red," said Oni. "And we're open to good ideas. If you have some suggestions, we encourage you to share them. We need the creativity and brainpower of everyone seated here because the bottom line is, whatever happens from this point on affects all of us."

After some initial hesitancy, various people began to raise their hands and put in their two cents. Some of the ideas were gems; some made Oni regret asking them to offer suggestions.

Jamal glanced over at Catt. "You're being mighty quiet over there, Miss Cason. Do you have any suggestions?"

Catt lifted her eyes. "I'll let you know when I come up with something brilliant."

Oni faced the group again. "Look, no one said that we had to get this done all in one day. I only intended for this to be a brainstorming session, and we've already gotten some great ideas out of it. Let's just go to lunch and pick this up again around two."

As they adjourned and began filing out, Catt picked up Oni's list and began skimming through it, mentally checking off the ideas that she liked most.

"Didn't you hear her say break for lunch?" asked Jamal over Catt's shoulder.

Catt jumped. "Why are you always sneaking up on me like that?"

"Why are you always so jumpy and tense? Do I make you nervous?"

"Yes, the same way murderers do when I'm alone on a dark street."

He feigned being shot in the heart. "That was cold!"

"It's a cold world," she snarled, dropping her pen and notebook into her bag.

Jamal's expression changed. "I want you to do me a favor."

Catt zipped her bag. "Don't worry. I already have. My father is a pastor. I took the liberty of asking him to add you to this week's prayer list. Now that I see you'll be gone for three weeks, it appears that my prayers have been answered."

"Yes, I'll be gone for three weeks. While I'm gone, I want you to try to get laid or get high or do whatever it takes to make you less of a pill by the time I get back."

She bristled at the suggestion. "You're not the easiest person to get along with either, Jamal. I know you've got these women hanging on to your every word, but they're not stuck down there in the lab with you. They don't know what's beyond the good looks and nice body."

He chuckled a bit. "At least that's some progress."

"What?"

"Hearing you acknowledge that you've noticed these good looks and this nice body. I was worried that you might be a lesbian."

Catt resented the notion. "What's the exact date you'll be leaving? This tour of yours can't come soon enough for me!"

"I'll be gone in a week. Try to find a way to live without me."

"Living without you isn't the problem. It's living *with* you—*that's* keeping me near the cross."

Jamal gave up. "Enjoy your lunch, Miss Cason."

Catt watched his retreating figure exit out the door. His leaving would be a welcomed relief and a blessing in disguise, she told herself. It was almost convincing enough to get her to believe that she wouldn't miss him.

Chapter 10

Oni rose from her desk and closed the door after summoning both Jamal and Catt to her office promptly at 10:00 in the morning. "Please have a seat."

Three days before Oni and Jamal were set to depart, Catt and Jamal both received a cryptic e-mail from Oni requesting their presence.

The two coworkers sat down in the two Riviera wood chairs in front of Oni's massive oak desk. Like everything else in the office, the chairs were sleek, elegant, and inspired envy, just like Oni.

"There's been a change of plans," announced Oni, drumming her fingers on the desk. "With everything that's going on, there's no way I can afford to take off for three weeks. I can't go on the road with you, Jamal."

His mouth fell open. "What?"

Oni flipped through her calendar. "Drea had her baby last night, four weeks early. This means that Chad is taking on some of her immediate responsibilities, and I've got to catch the slack for him. I just found out that I've got to take his meeting with some of our people out in California next week. Plus, we just had another chemist quit on top of everything else that's going on. It's impossible for me to get away right now."

"But everything is already set!" he protested in an almost whiny tone. "We've secured venues, set everything up with the marketing team, and already sent out press releases. To cancel it at the last minute like this would be a huge mistake, Oni—a mistake that Telegenic can't afford to make right now."

Catt backed him up. "Jamal's right, Oni. The company has been planning this for weeks. It'll ruin our credibility if we back out now."

Oni nodded and clasped her hands together. "I know. I totally agree with you, and I'm glad to know that you feel so strongly about it, Catt. It really helps to know that you're on board with supporting this project."

"Of course, I am. I want to see Telegenic thrive, just like everyone else." She eyed Jamal curiously. Had he told Oni something that would make her question Catt's loyalty to the company?

"So then it's settled," concluded Jamal, relieved. "We're still going to go out and do this promotional tour as planned."

"Yes and no." Oni eased from behind her desk and stood in front of them. "Jamal, I never said I was canceling the tour; I just said I couldn't go with you," she clarified.

Jamal adjusted his position in the chair, visibly distressed. "Oni, I mean, I'll do my best, but it's a pretty big job for one person to take on . . ."

Oni propped up against her desk. "It is. That's why I asked Catt to meet with us today."

"What does all this have to do with me?" asked Catt as the pieces started to fall into place, much to her dismay. "No, you don't mean—"

Realizing the implication, Jamal was just as distraught as Catt was. "Oni, I know you don't want Catt and me to—"

"The two of you carrying out the tour together makes perfect sense!" reasoned Oni. "You already work together and have camaraderie with each other. You know the product better than anyone else in the office, and you can be working on other projects in between promoting the new line. It's perfect."

"Oni, you and I already had a set plan," pointed out Jamal. "We've been putting this whole thing together since I started here. Catt barely knows what's going on!"

"So you'll brief her and bring her up to speed," directed Oni.

"The tour kicks off Thursday. I can't get ready to leave for three weeks in three days," Catt bemoaned.

"Sure you can. In fact, I'm giving you the rest of the week off to start packing and getting things in order. I also want you to use this time to review the products and the marketing strategy. The company can not afford to have either of you screw this up."

Jamal stood up, pleading with her to reconsider. "But, Oni, think about—"

Oni cleared her throat and stared him down, enunciating slowly. "Perhaps I didn't make myself clear," said Oni in an inflection that meant it was going to be her way or the highway. "I'm not going on the tour. I have too many obligations here to take that kind of time off. You, on the other hand, Jamal, will go on as scheduled. Catt will be joining you. I will check in with the two of you every day and fly in for a couple of stops when I can. All of the arrangements have already been made for you. Catt, all you have to do is give your plants to the neighbors to water and toss some clothes in a suitcase."

They both stood silently, lips pressed together and refusing to say anything to defy Oni. As cool as she was, she was still their boss.

"Are there any questions or concerns?" she asked. "Speak now or forever hold your peace."

Catt inched up her hand. "I just need a copy of the itinerary to look over and to give to my dad. I don't want him to be worried and wondering where I am."

"No problem. You can get all of that from Michelle. Anything else?"

Jamal shook his head. Catt looked down at the patterns in the tile.

"Cheer up, you two!" She slapped Jamal on the arm. "You're about to go on the adventure of a lifetime, not to the electric chair!"

Catt raised her eyes. "Is that an option?"

"No," replied Oni. She pulled Catt off to the side, out of earshot from Jamal. "This is a great opportunity for you. You're due for some fun in your life. This is a business trip, but no one said it had to be *all* business . . ."

Catt wrinkled her nose. "What are you trying to say?"

Oni cut her eyes to Jamal. "I'm trying to say that you're going to be alone out on the open road with a very attractive, very eligible man for the next few weeks. I would make the most it. Heck, I had planned to if I didn't have to cancel at the last minute."

"If I didn't know better, I'd think you were trying to encourage me to hit the sheets with Jamal!" replied Catt in a stern whisper.

"I'm not telling you to do that. I'm telling you to live a little and enjoy yourself. Jamal is the kind of guy who's great for that sort of thing."

"Oni, did you pray before making this decision?" Oni groaned loudly. "I'm serious! How do we know it's the Lord's will for me to go out on the road for three weeks with a man I hardly even know?"

"It's *the company's* will! And it's *your* will to stay gainfully employed, which could be in serious jeopardy if we don't see a spike in sales real soon. Please don't turn this into some religious event, Catt. Just say you'll go."

Catt relented. "Okay, okay! You win. It's not like I have much choice in the matter anyway."

"You don't, but you could've been a real witch about having to go. I'm glad you chose not to be. And I really do want you and Jamal to have some fun while you're out there on the road. This trip doesn't have to be a grudge."

Catt shook her head. "The last thing I need is to be mixing business and pleasure with a player like Jamal."

"Suit yourself. Either way, you're going on this trip. You might as well make it one to remember."

Chapter 11

Three days later, Catt found herself staring out of the window of Jamal's shiny black Suburban as he backed out of her driveway.

"Turn left," directed the automated voice through the GPS system. It was the first of many directives sure to follow during the 200 miles of highways and back roads they had to cover that day. Catt wondered if the monotonous voice would be the only semblance of conversation they'd encounter for the duration of the trip. She had nothing to say to him, and he had even less to say to her. There was little else to do but sit back, delve into her new Michelle McKinney Hammond book, and pray that the time passed quickly.

Accordingly, there was no shortage of prayers being lifted on Catt's behalf. When she announced her imminent departure to her father, he immediately recruited a group of prayer warriors to encircle her and cover her in prayer. The unspoken concern was not that Catt would be out of town for nearly a month, but that she would be out of town with a strapping young man. Catt led a disciplined, God-directed life, but Jeremiah knew that she was subject to falling into temptation and sin just like everyone else. Some divine intervention could always put a crutch in the devil's plan before it had a chance to surface.

Toria, on the other hand, was a little more practical. Her going away present to Catt was a free hairdo along with a box of condoms.

"Just in case . . ." Toria cautioned her.

Catt balked at the idea of sleeping with Jamal and left the condoms at the hair salon.

After nearly five minutes of driving in silence, Jamal was the first to speak. "You wanna stop and get something to eat?" he asked without looking at her.

"Just because I'm a big girl doesn't mean I'm always hungry," Catt replied, then held in her stomach, daring it to growl and contradict her.

He cringed. "I just asked. I don't plan on stopping until we need gas or until we get to Philly, whichever comes first."

She rolled her eyes. "What if I have to pee?"

"There are some paper cups in the back. Knock yourself out."

Catt turned the page in her book and eyed the GPS. They had only gone seven miles, and she was already ready to strangle him.

"You wanna stop or what?" he asked again as they approached a chain of fast-food restaurants.

"I don't care."

He sighed heavily and pulled into the Waffle House parking lot. "We're not going to be in here all day," he warned her, thrusting the gear into park. "Just long enough for some coffee and an omelet."

"Don't I get a say in the matter?" asked Catt as she climbed out of the car.

"No."

After they sat down and placed their orders, the conversation that passed between them was limited to terse statements and one-word answers. Catt knew that if the next three weeks were going to be bearable, it would be up to her to at least make an effort to be cordial to Jamal.

She took a deep breath and said, "Tell me something I don't know about you."

He didn't look up from his scattered hash browns. "I don't like to talk while I'm eating."

She smacked her teeth and stirred cream into her coffee. "I'm just trying to make conversation."

"No one asked you to do that."

"I just think that we should get to know each other better, don't you?"

"We work together all day, every day. We already know everything we need to know."

"Not really. For instance, what's your favorite food? When's your birthday? What college did you go to?"

"Catt, I'm not about to play twenty-one Questions with you. That's some adolescent, high school mess. I've got better things to do."

"Like what?" she asked defiantly, cutting her pecan waffle into bite-sized pieces. "What better things do you have to do for the next three weeks than deal with me?"

"Look, I've got a lot on my mind right now. I've got at least four hours of driving ahead of me; I've got to make sure everything is ready for this first stop; and I've got to deal with a self-righteous, Bible-thumping know-it-all for the next three weeks. I just want to enjoy these last few minutes of peace I have right now."

Catt was thinking of a snappy comeback when her cell phone rang. She answered it, grateful for the interruption. "Hello?"

"Hey, Catt, it's me, Eldon . . . Minister James."

"Hey, Eldon, what's up?"

"Your dad just reminded me that you're leaving today. I wanted to let you know that I'm praying for you to have a safe journey, and I'm counting the minutes until you get back."

"That's sweet of you to say. Now, admit it—did my father put you up to calling me?"

"He didn't have to. I told you . . . I like you, Catt. I'm really hoping that you'll let me take you out to dinner when you get home."

Catt smiled into the phone. She was happy to have something to look forward to while she endured the road trip from hell. "Sure, Eldon. I'd like that."

"Then it's a date!" he confirmed. "We can work out the details when you get back. Call me when you get to your destination. I think I'll sleep better knowing that you got there safely."

"Will do," she assured him. "I'll talk to you later."

Jamal cut his eyes toward her and stopped chewing for a second. "Was that your boyfriend?"

"Why?"

He swallowed. "I'm just shocked that you'd even have a man."

"And I'm shocked that they let dogs like you roam the streets without a leash, so we're even."

Jamal laughed to himself. "I'm even more curious about the kind of man who'd date you. He must have low self-esteem. You seem like the type who would do that to a brother."

"Jamal, you would really be doing both of us a huge favor if you stopped pretending like you know me. You don't!"

"I may not know you all that well, but I know your type." He chewed his omelet. "I'm an expert on women."

She shot him a blank stare. "Oh, I know this'll be *too* funny! Please, enlighten me, Mr. Ford. Amaze me with your candor and wisdom regarding the fairer sex."

He wiped his mouth. "I will." Jamal turned to Catt and gave her the once-over. "You're the classic over-achiever. I bet you got all A's in school, probably were the captain of the debate team, president of the Honor Society. You didn't date much—too busy hitting the books and hiding snack cakes under your pillow. But you secretly longed to be the cheerleader or the popular girl in school who had all the guys drooling. Even now, you make the big dollars and get to push people around at work, but you're still lonely. You're still that insecure fifteen-year-old who wanted nothing more than for the cute basketball player to ask her to the prom or to even notice that she existed."

"Wow . . ." said Catt in amazement.

"Hit it right on the head, didn't I?" he asked smugly.

Catt nodded slowly. "It's incredible . . . you're an even bigger idiot than I thought!"

"What?"

"You're right. I was the captain—of the *cheerleading squad*, not the debate team! And I didn't spend my nights with my nose in some book. It just came naturally to me. I spent my nights with my sorors having fun and partying like everyone else. And I had a man, who, ironically, *was* a basketball player. We were together for three years, and *I* dumped *him* when I realized that I was too fabulous to settle for anything less than God's best. So you can take your little theory about me and *shove* it!" She flung one of her napkins at him.

"I bet there's at least a little truth to it," boasted Jamal. "Like I said, I know women."

"Really? Then why are you still single?"

"You mean other than the fact that I choose to be? For starters, most women don't even make it past the thirty-Day Plan."

She squinted her eyes. "The *what?*"

"The thirty-Day Plan. It's a system I've developed when it comes to dating. It's how I determine if I want to wife 'em or one-night 'em."

"What, pray tell, does this system consist of?" she asked sarcastically.

"It's a series of little tests to judge the important things. You know, how well a woman can hold a conversation and if she knows when to shut up. Does she have a stable job, is she too clingy or needy, have her head right and her *brain* right, if you know what I mean. Things like that."

Catt rolled her eyes. "Those are the *important* things?"

"Well, I mean, she's got to be gorgeous too," he noted.

She waited for more. "And that's it?"

"That's enough."

"Says who?"

"Any warm-blooded, straight male." Jamal mashed the remaining omelet into what was left of his hash browns. "Do you have a better guide for finding a wife?"

"Yes, the Bible."

He groaned and threw down his fork. "There you go again . . ."

"So you don't believe in the Bible?"

"If I say 'no,' are you going to sic Daddy on me?"

"If you don't believe in God and the Bible, my father will be the least of your problems, you heathen!"

Jamal held up his hands. "Relax, all right? I believe in God and the Bible and all that, but I'm also practical."

"What's more practical than desiring a woman of noble character, handles her business, makes her own money, feeds both the poor and her own family, keeps her man happy, knows when and when not to talk, and loves the Lord?"

"Tell me where I can find that chick!"

"In the Bible, specifically in Proverbs," replied Catt. "I've just describe the virtuous woman."

"I thought we were talking about women who actually exist."

"She does exist, but you'll never find her with that stupid thirty-Day Plan of yours."

Jamal pointed at Catt with his fork. "Don't knock the plan, Catt. I've dodged a lot of bullets using that system."

"You mean like Miss Missing Panties?"

He chuckled. "Yvette is a nice li'l package. She's sexy, smart, a lady in the streets but a freak in the sheets. It doesn't get much better than that."

"And where are she and her panties on the Plan?"

"Day eighteen, passed the halfway mark. I'm surprised you didn't recognize her. She models for J. Crew sometimes."

"A model—what a surprise," she replied drily. "And this is what attracted you to her?"

"You haven't seen her naked, Catt. Her body is the truth!"

Catt sprinkled salt on her grits. "It all sounds a little shallow to me."

Jamal corrected her. "What you're saying is *I* sound a little shallow to you, right?"

"I just think your criterion is a little superficial. It's all about looks and sex."

"I said good conversation too," he interjected.

"But looks seem to be a huge part of the equation. The Bible says charm is deceptive and beauty is fleeting. It goes on to say, 'Your beauty should not come from outward adornment . . . Rather, it should be that of your inner self, the unfading beauty of a gentle and quiet spirit, which is of great worth in God's sight.' I wouldn't get so hung up on the exterior if I were you."

"You're not me."

"What if you met a woman who was smart, funny, who stimulated you mentally and figuratively, but she wasn't exactly gorgeous? Would you give her a shot?"

"Depends . . . what does her body look like?"

Catt hesitated. "She's my size."

Silence passed between them again. Then Jamal admitted, "I don't think I'd be physically attracted to a larger woman."

"So it doesn't matter how smart she is or . . . if she doesn't look like Halle Berry's twin sister, you're not interested."

"I didn't say all that."

"But that's what you meant. Men like you miss out on your blessings every day just because women don't come wrapped the way you think they should. Besides, who's to say that dime you're so obsessed with won't turn into a fat quarter a few meals and babies down the road?"

"Whatever! You're still single, so what does your Bible have to say about that?"

"It says, 'The Lord Almighty has sworn, surely, as I have planned, so it will be, and as I have purposed, so it will stand.' My husband will come according to God's timing, not mine. Having a man isn't my priority right now anyway. Having a man fall in love with this new fragrance and buying a ton of it for his lady is."

Jamal balled up his napkin and tossed it onto the tray. "I hear ya!"

"And if we're going to find these men willing to drop their hard-earned paychecks on Telegenic products, we better get out of here," advised Catt, sliding out of the booth.

Jamal grabbed his car keys and stood up. "All right, Miss Catt Cason. Let the adventure begin!"

Chapter 12

"Well, that's one city down, nine more to go," said Jamal, hopping into the SUV after filling it with gas. Their first stop had been met with moderate success. They hadn't changed the world, but most patrons stopped at their mall station long enough to indulge in a few of Telegenic's upcoming products, give critical feedback, and be added to the company's e-mail list.

He revved up the engine. "You know, I wouldn't be offended if you offered to drive every once in a while."

"I'll keep that in mind." Catt toyed with the radio. "I wish we knew some good stations out here."

"You were the one who insisted I take out my iPod."

"Forgive me for not wanting to endure another three hours of Jay-Z's greatest hits. A girl can only take so much!" Catt frowned as she switched from country to rock to talk radio. "There's nothing on that I want to hear."

"If you're looking for the gospel station, let me save you the trouble. As long as I'm driving, we're going to listen to what I want to hear. John P. Kee, Kirk Franklin, and all of them are not on today's playlist."

"Is this what you want to hear?" she asked, pausing at Al B. Sure's '80s hit, "Nite and Day."

Jamal turned up the radio and nodded his head. "I'd forgotten all about this song." A smile spread across his lips, as if the song triggered some pleasant memory. "Yeah, this was the jam back in the day. We had some good times off this song."

Catt raised an eyebrow. "*We?*"

He laughed a little. "Yeah, me and this chick named Meka. She loved this song. She liked to play it whenever . . . you know."

"Whenever what?"

He grinned. "Whenever she was in the mood."

"Oh, was Meka your first love?"

"More like my first lover."

"*Humph*, I'm surprised you can even remember that many women back."

"I'll admit, I don't remember every name and every face, but I do remember Meka. She's the reason I have a special place in my heart for older women."

"How old was she?"

"Seventeen."

"How old were you?"

"Twelve or thirteen."

Catt gasped. "Twelve!"

"Yeah, Meka was the babysitter. She lived across the street."

"That's sick, Jamal! What would a practically grown woman see in a twelve-year-old?"

"I was a little big for my age. Besides, there's no age limitation on game and swag. Even at twelve, I had both."

"Yes, but there *are* law limitations on sex with children. She should've been arrested!"

Jamal frowned. "Why are you trying to make it seem like she was some kind of pedophile?"

"Because she was!"

"It wasn't like that," he recalled dreamily.

"I'm almost afraid to ask what it was like."

He smirked. "But you're dying to know, aren't you?"

"No."

He laughed. "Stop lying. If you quit acting so sanctimonious for two minutes, I might tell you."

She sucked her teeth in defiance, but she didn't say anything. He was right: she *was* dying to know what happened.

"It was like this," he regaled. "Meka used to come over to babysit when my mom had to work late. I told my mom I was too old for a babysitter, but she insisted on it because the neighborhood we lived in wasn't all that safe. Anyway, one night, Meka came over when I was already in the bed asleep. She crept into the room and started touching on me. It caught me off guard, but Meka was fine so I wasn't about to tell her to stop. When she saw that I was awake, she asked me if I wanted to touch her too."

"What did you say?"

"I didn't say anything. I let my fingers do the talking. Next thing I knew, Meka was taking off her clothes and gave me the best three minutes of my life . . . up until that time at least. I never complained about having a babysitter after that."

"Did you tell anybody?"

"I told my cousin Bone. He was fifteen. After I told him, he asked her about it and she ended up giving him some too. She kept both of us very happy. She and Bone ended up having a kid together." He sighed. "Good ol' Meka . . ."

Catt shook her head in disbelief. "I don't believe you."

"You don't have to."

"Do you know what I was doing at that age? Still playing with Barbie dolls and playing kickball outside with my friends. Sex was nowhere on the menu."

"I was into sports and all that too, but after Meka showed me the light . . ." Jamal shook his head. "It was like, 'Forget football. *This* is the best thing out there!' Chasing girls became my favorite sport from then on."

Catt became serious. "How can you not see that both you and your cousin were victims of sexual abuse?"

"Call it what you want, Catt. All I know is this song is making me want to give Meka a call right now." He began to sing along in bad falsetto.

"If this story is true, it certainly explains a lot. I see now why you have such a dysfunctional way of relating to women. I think that's often true with abuse victims."

"Whatever." He turned down the music a little as Al B. Sure faded into a song by Howard Hewitt. "What about you?"

"What about me?"

"I told you about my first time." He nudged her with his elbow. "Go on and spill the tea about yours."

"I didn't ask you to divulge that information. In fact, I'm wishing you hadn't."

"You didn't seem to have a problem with my sordid tale of lust and underage sex while you were listening to it." He thought about it. "Then again, I forgot you're a preacher's kid. Is there even a losing virginity story to tell?"

"Are you asking if I've ever had sex?"

Jamal turned to her. "Have you?"

She averted eye contact with him. "You're very nosey, Jamal."

"Hey, we're going to be on the road for a long time. According to you, we might as well make the time pass by getting to know each other, right?"

Catt was quiet and stared out of the window.

"Well . . ." egged on Jamal.

"Well, what?"

"I'm waiting. Are you a virgin or not?"

She exhaled, embarrassed and annoyed. "No."

Jamal perked up, amused. "Oh, so Daddy's little girl isn't as innocent she wants everybody to think she is.

Does the bishop know you've been lettin' some dude tap that?"

"My father and I don't discuss my sex life."

Jamal was shocked. "There's a whole sex life?"

Catt shook her head. "I'm *so* not getting into this with you!"

"Come on now, stop being bashful. Everybody in this car is grown, and I'm not going to run out and tell Pastor Daddy that his daughter likes to get her groove on every now and then."

"Shut up, Jamal." Catt opened her book and pretended to read.

"Okay, I promise to be as quiet as a mouse while you tell me about your first time."

She turned to him with a scowl on her face. "Why do you even care?"

"Why are you making it such a big deal? Are you ashamed because you didn't wait until your wedding night?"

"You should be ashamed too!" she squealed.

"I'll tell you what—we can both repent after you tell the story, so spill it. Who was he?"

Catt sighed and closed the book. She still refused to look at him. "His name was Stanley Johnson," she said at last.

"*Stanley?* You gave it up to a dude named Stanley? I can already tell he was lame. How old were you?"

"We were both sixteen."

Jamal sighed. "Ah, freak-sixteen! I remember those days . . ."

"We were not freaks, at least I wasn't."

"I'll be the judge of that. So what happened?"

"Stanley was a boy I met at church, my first real boyfriend. He was real sweet and very quiet, very serious about reading the Word and understanding the Lord."

"He couldn't have been too serious if he deflowered you."

"Well, he loved the Lord, but he was still a teenage boy with raging hormones."

"I see."

"Anyway, we would read the Bible together sometimes. One day, he came over to my house. My parents trusted me, and they really trusted him, so they didn't mind him coming over even if they weren't home. On this particular day, we were reading The Song of Songs to each other."

"What's that?"

"It's a book of love songs between Solomon and a Shulammite woman. It's very romantic."

"Romantic Bible verses?" he asked incredulously.

"Yes. He says things to her like, 'Your navel is a rounded goblet . . . Your waist is a mound of wheat encircled by lilies. Your breasts are like two fawns, like twins of a gazelle.'"

Jamal glanced over at Catt. "That's that Old Testament game right there! I may have to add that one to my collection."

"I guess all that talk about legs and breasts and Solomon tasting the choice fruits of the woman's garden were just too much for Stanley. This was pretty erotic stuff for two sheltered sixteen-year-olds."

"That's a little erotic at any age. Maybe I *should* be reading the Bible more."

"As we were reading, I noticed Stanley kind of looking at me with this strange twinkle in his eyes, like it was the first time he realized that I wasn't just his sister in Christ but a developing young woman. The more we read, the hotter the room got. By the time we got to, 'My beloved thrust his hand through the latch-opening, my heart began to pound for him,' we just couldn't take it anymore."

"Are you sure this is in the Bible?"

"Yes, I can't make this stuff up! We were so fired up that everything we believed about chastity and waiting for marriage was out the window. For that moment, he was Solomon, I was the Shulammite woman, and we got it poppin' in the garden, or rather, the air mattress in our basement."

Jamal howled with laughter. "Who loses their virginity while reading the Bible?"

Catt stomped her foot. "It's *not* funny, Jamal!"

"All right, I'm sorry," he apologized, still recovering from laughing. "What happened after that?"

"We both felt so guilty afterward that we spent the next two hours in prayer and repentance. Stanley never came back to my house after that, and I stuck to reading David and Goliath or Daniel in the lion's den."

"Wow . . . this is the first time I've ever heard of the Bible getting people *into* trouble."

Catt shuddered, still mortified by the entire ordeal. "Believe me, it's not my proudest moment!"

"Did you tell your parents?"

"Are you serious? Did you tell yours about Meka?"

"And mess up a good thing? No way!" he chuckled. "So was that the first and last time?"

"With Stanley?"

"With anybody."

"Maybe . . ." She winked her eye at him. "Maybe not."

Jamal looked at her with a new appreciation. "You're not as prudish as I thought. I bet there's no telling how many surprises and secrets you've got in that head of yours."

Instead of disputing it, Catt played coy and flipped open her book. "It's a long way to New York." She reclined the seat back. "No need to tell all my secrets within the first three days."

"So it gets juicier than Bible sex with Stanley?"

Catt bared a sly smile. "Boy, you have *no* idea!"

Chapter 13

Silver Springs, Maryland, was on the agenda for the day. Both Jamal and Catt had worked up an appetite catching whiffs of cooked delights floating in from the food court as they started the round of customer presentations and promotions for the day. By 2:00, both were ready to eat just about anything that could be steamed, fried, baked, or broiled.

Jamal took Catt to a European-style bistro across the street from the mall. "After you," he said, holding the door open for Catt.

In jest, she curtsied and smiled, then walked through it. "Thank you, kind sir."

A waiter led them to a table almost immediately.

"By the way, I liked the way you handled yourself with those customers today," he noted. "I've been watching you. You can go from being a little flirty with the men to being that sista-friend with the ladies to being 'grandbaby' to the seniors without batting an eye or breaking a sweat. I'm starting to see that there's a lot more to you than you let on to the rest of the world, isn't there?" guessed Jamal after they'd placed their drink orders.

"Sometimes what you see isn't always what you get," she hinted.

"I guess we never had an official get-to know-each-other-Q-and-A session since you pretty much dissed me when we first met."

"I wasn't that bad," scoffed Catt. "Even if I was, it wasn't like you didn't deserve it. You were a complete jerk from the moment I first laid eyes on you."

"Well, I'm human. And if I remember correctly, you weren't too welcoming yourself. You did try to get me fired, after all," recalled Jamal. They both laughed.

"You didn't let that deter you."

"No, I didn't. Something about you struck me the second I saw you," said Jamal, looking at her intently. "I knew you were something different."

The waitress came by with their drinks, and they placed their food orders.

"Anyway, I don't want to talk about work anymore," began Jamal once the waitress left. "I want to talk about you."

"What about me?" she asked, stirring sugar into her tea.

"For starters, where are you from? How old are you? Tell me about your family, your hobbies. Do you have a man, any kids?"

"I was born in Jacksonville, but we moved to Charlotte when I was still an infant. It's the only place I've ever considered home."

He nodded. "Okay, that's a start. How old are you?"

"You're not supposed to ask a woman her age, Jamal. Being a player, I thought you knew that."

"I'm not playing right now. I'm sitting here trying to get to know you."

"I just turned thirty-one. What about you?"

"I'm thirty-six and a Scorpio. What do you like to do? There's got to be more to you than church and Telegenic."

"There is. I enjoy reading and singing. Believe it or not, I'm actually a bit of a sports fanatic."

"Really?"

"Yeah, I love sports—except basketball. I suck at basketball. I like basically everything that has to do with the outdoors. I love to travel too."

"Do you get to travel much?"

"Sometimes, in fact, I just got back from Belize right before you started working at Telegenic."

"Belize, huh? Must be nice."

"Oh, it was! I went snorkeling for the first time, jungle cruising, trekking through the rainforest. And the beaches were just breathtaking, especially at Ambergris Caye where I was staying."

"It sounds wonderful, but it doesn't seem like the kind of place that a person goes to alone."

She sipped her drink. "I never said that I went by myself."

"Oh, so you *do* have a man."

"No, I don't have a boyfriend. I went with a few friends of mine. We spent a year planning for that trip." He looked puzzled. "What?"

"Nothing . . . I just never pictured you having friends."

"I have friends, Jamal, and, occasionally, I even have boyfriends! I told you, you don't know me as well as you think you do."

"All right, so tell me about these boyfriends of yours."

"Well, I haven't had a serious relationship in a while, not since Greg." Her ex-fiancé was not a subject Catt was eager to discuss, especially not with Jamal. "What about you? Do you think you'll ever stop philandering long enough to settle down?"

"I don't know. I think all that love and romance crap is overrated."

"Is this the voice of someone who's had his heart broken?"

"*Please!* You have to give someone your heart in order for them to break it, and I don't intend to do that."

"Admit it, Jamal. I know you've had your heart broken at least once." She leaned into him. "So who is she?"

"See, you want to know too much too soon. Time in the lab with you has proven to me that patience is not one of your virtues, but you're going to have to pretend like it is for now. You don't need to know all of my secrets yet."

Catt sat back. "It's no secret that you'd made quite a name for yourself at Mystique. How did you end up at Telegenic?"

"Fate, I guess. Plus, the chance at more autonomy and responsibilities was an offer I couldn't refuse."

"Where were you before that?"

"At this start-up company in Paris. That's where I learned most of my tricks of the trade. Paris is a great place to cut your teeth in this business."

"Paris? As in France?"

"Why do you sound so surprised?"

"Because you look about as 'hood' as it gets! I can't imagine you traipsing around Europe."

"See, you don't know all there is to know about me either."

"I guess not."

"France was cool. I lived there for a couple of years. After I came back to the States, I knew that I wanted to move back to the South. A friend of mine from school had just landed a job at Mystique, and she knew I was looking to settle down here, so she hooked me up with the right people at the company, and the rest is history."

The waitress returned and set their plates down in front of them.

"This looks delicious!" said Catt, tossing her festive mix of oranges, spinach, and avocado in her pork tenderloin salad. Jamal frowned. "What?" she asked, looking up at him.

"Nothing, I just don't eat pork, that's all—beef, pork, none of that stuff that's going to clog my heart in a few years."

"You're a vegan?"

"No, I do eat seafood, sometimes chicken. I just try to lay off the red meat."

"I didn't know you were so health-conscious."

"Add that to the growing list of things you don't know about me."

Catt bit into her salad. "I understand your wanting to protect your heart, but believe me—some things are worth having a heart attack! This is one of them." She took a moment to savor the taste and gestured her head toward his plate. "Of course, you're not faring too much better over there with all of that cheese and mushroom sauce smothered across your polenta."

She swallowed her food. "So was it Meka?" goaded Catt.

"Was who Meka?"

"The woman who broke your heart."

"I thought that we weren't going to talk about that," he reminded her while slicing his food.

"You thought wrong."

Jamal sighed and set down his fork and knife. "Dang, you're getting all up in my business today, aren't you?"

"You're the one who said that we needed to have a get-to-know-you session, so this is all a part of my getting to know you. Now, back to my question, if it wasn't Meka, then who was it that broke your heart?"

"I don't want to talk about that right now. Next question, please."

Catt thought for a moment. "Are you happy?"

Jamal looked down at his plate. "I don't know."

"Why not?"

"Happiness is one of those metaphysical things. There's no one answer. Am I happy right now? Yeah, for the most part, but that could change five minutes from now. There's no set answer."

"I think there is," asserted Catt. "You're right; happiness can be fleeting. Joy, the kind that comes from the Lord, is always present."

"I have yet to experience that. Then again, I'm positive I've gone through some things that you have yet to experience."

"Are you about to reveal one of your many secrets?" inquired Catt.

"I don't have secrets, I have skeletons. In fact, my skeletons have skeletons!"

"Now I'm really intrigued." At that moment, the waitress came over and asked if they wanted anything else. They both declined.

"Are you sure that you don't want anything else?" asked Jamal after she left.

"I do have a figure to watch. I've got to admit, though, a little of that chocolate hazelnut tart would hit the spot right about now."

"Why don't you order one? If you feel guilty about the calories, you can work it off later. There's a gym inside the hotel."

"It's tempting, but I can't. Chocolate always goes right to one place on me," she said, balling up her napkin.

"Where's that?" he asked, smiling.

"I'm sitting on it."

He tilted his head to the side. "Well, from what I've seen, the chocolate has been doing its job."

"I thought you didn't find big girls attractive."

"I don't, and I never said that the chocolate was doing a *good* job." He drew his hands up in mock defense. "I'm teasing, okay? Don't shoot me!"

"Contrary to what you think, I *can* take a joke, Jamal." She bit her lip. "Besides, I look in the mirror. I know I need to lose some weight."

"I think you need to be healthy, but lose the weight—don't lose yourself in the process."

"But I guess a man like you goes for the skinny-minny variety."

"She doesn't have to be a skinny minny although I do have a penchant for modelesque."

"Haven't you ever heard the phrase 'bigger is better'?"

"It depends on *what's* bigger." Catt shot him a look of contempt.

"Don't look at me like that! Do you mean to tell me that you have no standards when it comes to looks in the opposite sex?"

"No."

"So you'd date anyone from a midget weighing twenty pounds to a giant weighing in at 400?"

"Yes, as long as his heart is right."

"Don't you think it's important to be physically attracted to someone?"

"I think it's important to be *spiritually* attracted."

Jamal groaned. "Cue Pastor Cason . . ."

"Well, it's true. You can marry the most beautiful woman in the world, but if the relationship does nothing to feed your spirit, what do you really have?"

"*The most beautiful woman in the world!*" he pointed out.

Catt looked at him with pity. "And that's what's truly sad. For all of your degrees and expertise and worldly wisdom, you're still one of the dumbest Negroes I know!"

Chapter 14

"These roads seem to go on forever," whined Catt, looking out of the window as Jamal drove them toward what seemed to be the middle of nowhere.

"According to the GPS, we should hit civilization in about an hour or so." Jamal's phone beeped, indicating an incoming text message. "Can you check that for me?"

"It's from Oni." She read the message. "She wants you to e-mail her the spec numbers or something like that. She says she deleted it by mistake."

"Okay, scroll through my phone and click on my e-mail account and forward the e-mail from Oni. It should have yesterday's date on it," instructed Jamal.

Catt began scrolling through the phone. "I see it." She forwarded the e-mail to Oni. The phone beeped again. "You've got another text. You want me to check it?"

"Yeah, it's probably Oni again to let me know she got it."

Catt looked at the message. A look of disgust swept over her face. "Eww, *what* is this?" she squealed. She held up the phone, which had a picture of a woman spread eagle on the screen.

He glanced at the picture with a simper. "You came equipped with one, so you know what it is. A more appropriate question would be *whose* it is."

"According to the message attached to it, it's yours." Catt frowned. She scanned through the other pictures in his phone, which included more naked and scantily clad women in various poses. "Do these women have no shame?"

"Why should they be ashamed of their bodies?"

"I didn't say they should be ashamed of their bodies, but they should be ashamed to send their genitals via text message."

"What's wrong with taking some sexy pics? It's fun."

"No, it's sleazy, and it's trashy."

Jamal smacked his teeth and eyed her with skepticism. "So you've never taken or received some buck-naked pictures?"

"No. That's disgusting. I don't like porn."

"It's not porn. It's . . . celebrating your sexuality."

"Are you serious? In this day and age, a picture like that could end up on the Internet or get forwarded to the wrong person. Before you know it, the whole world will know things only your gynecologist is supposed to be privy to!"

"You have to be selective about who you send them to, and if they're really racy, you don't put your face in the shot."

She rejected either option. "I don't need coaching in proper naked picture etiquette, thank you very much."

He snatched his phone back from her and began dialing. "You're way too uptight, Catt. What's so terrible about embracing your sexuality and injecting a little fun into your life?"

"I try to live holy, Jamal. Taking nasty pictures and sending them to my friends isn't part of that process." Her phone vibrated. She checked it and her eyes widened to the size of saucers. She abruptly ejected the phone from her hands. "*Eww!*"

Jamal howled, laughing.

Catt looked down at the image on the phone in horror and a little fascination. "Oh my God, is that you?"

Jamal nodded. "Impressive, isn't it?"

Catt covered her hands with her face. "Oh my God, why did you send me that? Why didn't you warn me?" She let down the window. "I think I'm going to be sick!"

Jamal laughed again. "Lighten up, C.C. I'm just having a little fun with you, that's all."

"Watching me suppress the urge to throw up through my eyeballs is your idea of fun? Why would you think my definition of fun would be getting flashed by pictures of your . . . *package!* Why do you even walk around with that in your phone?"

"For moments like this," he retorted.

"Is *this* what you show women when you meet them? Is giving a woman your business card considered passé now?"

"It's my way of giving 'em something to look forward to."

Catt shook her head piteously. "You're such a pervert!"

Jamal took his eyes off the road for a moment to watch her. "Look at you all out of breath over there. Are you in shock or intrigued?"

"Are you kidding me? That's way more of you than I ever wanted to see." She picked up the phone and promptly hit Delete. But not before taking one last glimpse. "Now, we can pretend that never happened, although I'm afraid that image may be permanently burned into my brain."

"Catt, every woman I know has taken at least one naughty picture of herself. You really need to try it. It's liberating."

She narrowed her eyes at him. "And exactly *who* would I be taking it for?"

"For you! It's an ego boost, like saying to the world, 'Yeah, I'm sexy, and I know it!'"

She shot her nose in the air. "I'm not that vain. Not to mention that I don't like looking at myself naked."

Jamal seemed shocked. "Why not?"

"Jamal, come on." She sighed. "You said yourself that I'm not what you'd consider modelesque."

"It doesn't matter what I think. I'm just some dude you work with. What matters is what *you* think."

"I don't think I'm ugly or anything like that. I just don't feel all that sexy, not with this extra weight on me," she confided to him.

"You can look good naked at any size. It's all about attitude." He thought for a moment. "I'll tell you what. When we check into the hotel, I want you to go into the bathroom, take all your clothes off, and take some pictures. I guarantee it'll give you a whole new lease on life."

Her mouth flew open. "Are you *serious?*"

"Shoot, yeah! It'll do you some good to tap into your inner Playboy bunny."

"I think I'll pass on that one. Once we check in, I intend to take a long, hot shower, finish reading Proverbs, and go to bed."

"Catt, I admire your commitment to Christ and holy living, I really do, but you've got to live a little sometimes. I keep telling you, there's a whole life outside the church and the office."

"I know that!" she snapped.

"Then act like it! While you're taking that shower, go on and take a picture."

"No, thanks. I'm not in the habit of doing things that I know I'm going to regret later."

"Don't say I never tried to help you bring sexy back," said Jamal.

Catt dozed off. When she awakened, Jamal was taking their luggage out of the truck and preparing to check into the hotel.

She stuck her head through the window and called to him. "You need some help?"

"I got it. Why don't you go on and get the room keys. I'll catch up with you in the lobby."

After getting them checked into separate rooms and agreeing to meet for dinner in the hotel's restaurant in an hour, Catt and Jamal parted ways.

Once in the room, Catt stripped down and turned the shower's hot water on full blast. She scrubbed away the grime and dirt of the day and emerged from the shower feeling like a new woman.

Catt caught a glimpse of her reflection in the mirror as she toweled off. She looked directly into the mirror, then turned for a profile view. Her body wasn't perfect, but her skin was smooth and tight. She admired the structure of her arms—thick but not flabby—and the roundness of her breasts. Her thighs had a little cellulite on them, but that was okay. She'd always loved her shapely golden legs, which hardly ever required shaving. No one could argue that she had a pretty face. She smiled at the image in the mirror. She actually looked good naked, good enough for a picture even.

Catt stealthily reached over to her phone lying on the sink. The thought of taking nude pictures was exhilarating, like running naked through the sprinkler.

She angled the cell phone in the mirror to take the most flattering position of herself. But she was nervous, and the first few shots came out too blurry. Eventually, with a steady hand, she'd taken one that didn't look half bad. It was kind of sexy. *She* was kind of sexy.

She posed in seductive positions like the women on Jamal's phone. Catt decided to take her newfound confidence and sexiness a step further. It was risky, but she was in that kind of mood. She snapped a picture of herself with her towel draped over her private parts but still revealing enough skin to know she wasn't wearing anything else. She went to "recent" on her phone and hit Jamal's number, giggling like a schoolgirl as she sent the picture to him. She figured he would get a kick out of the picture and even more, that she had the nerve to follow through with taking it. The giggles, however, quickly turned to gasps when the phone registered a message that read "Successfully sent to Daddy."

"*What? No!*" she cried. She frantically searched through the phone trying to see what went wrong. It soon became apparent that her nervous hand accidentally pressed her father's name instead of Jamal's.

"Oh my God! Oh, Jesus! This is not happening!" she wailed. She glanced at the picture again and cringed when she thought about what her father's reaction would be to seeing it.

Catt threw on a T-shirt and jeans and hightailed it to Jamal's room across the hall. She banged on the door with the force of a SWAT team.

Jamal swung open the door. "Are you crazy? What's wrong with you, beating on my door like that?"

Catt shoved him aside and barged into the room. "You're such as idiot, Jamal! I can't believe I listened to you!"

"What?"

Catt slammed the door shut. "I took those stupid pictures like you told me to."

Jamal beamed and gave her two thumbs-up. "Good for you! So what's the problem?"

She huffed and puffed as she paced the floor. "I knew listening to you could only result in disaster!"

"Calm down! Why you got your panties all in a bunch?"

She snorted. "That's a little hard to do considering that I wasn't wearing any!"

Jamal sat down on the bed. "Now, you've got me *really* interested. What happened?"

Catt took a deep breath. "Like I said, I took the freakin' pictures!"

"And?" he pushed.

She sat down next to him. "And I tried to send one to you—just for laughs, that's it!"

His eyes bulged. "For real?" He promptly began scrolling through his phone.

She covered her face with her hands, mortified. "Except I sent it to my dad by mistake!"

Jamal roared with laughter. "You did *what?*"

"I was nervous and hit the wrong name," explained Catt. She fumed watching him laugh. "Shut up, Jamal! It's not funny!"

"You're right. It's hilarious!"

She punched him in the arm. "This is all your fault, you know."

"Wait a minute. I only told you to take the pictures. I didn't say anything about sending them."

"I guess I got caught up in the moment," said Catt in a small voice.

Jamal grinned at her. "But it felt good, didn't it?"

"Yeah, it did," she admitted—"until I realized I sent pictures of my breasts to my father. I feel completely humiliated right now."

"I wouldn't worry about it. Just tell him your phone was hacked or something."

"You want me to lie?"

"Do you want to tell him the truth? That you were taking freaky pictures to send to me?"

Catt thought it over. "You have a point. Perhaps honesty isn't the best policy in this case," she conceded.

Jamal placed a hand on her shoulder. "The important thing to remember here is that you got outside your comfort zone. You did something impetuous and discovered something about yourself you didn't know before."

She exhaled. "I guess I can look at it that way."

"And speaking of looking," his lips curved into a mischievous smirk, "you gon' let me see those pictures or what?"

"No!" shrieked Catt. "Nobody's ever going to see those pictures!"

"Except your dad, you mean."

She sucked her teeth. "Very funny."

"Maybe not so much right now, but I guarantee you're going to look back on this and laugh," he assured her.

"That day can't come soon enough!" Catt was startled by her phone vibrating. She grimaced when she looked at the caller ID. "I guess we don't have to wonder whether my dad got the picture."

"Why do you say that?"

"Because it's him!"

Chapter 15

Jeremiah hung up the phone with a puzzled look on his face. First, there was the scintillating picture of his daughter that he received via a picture-message on his phone. If that wasn't shocking enough—and it was—Catt's bungled explanation for it was a blatant lie.

"I think someone hacked into my phone and sent it," she'd told him. When asked if someone had stolen her phone, then returned it, she said no, then yes, then that she wasn't sure.

"But you did take the picture, right?" he asked her.

To that, she claimed that she must've snapped it by accident after taking a shower.

"Let me get this straight," he continued, "you *accidentally* took a naked picture, which happens to look posed for, and then someone stole your phone, sent the picture to your father, and then returned the phone with you being none the wiser. Is *that* what you're saying happened?"

Apparently it was.

Jeremiah wasn't positive, but he was almost sure that he heard a man in the background coaching her on what to say. Presumably, it was the guy she'd been traveling with. He was never too keen on the idea of Catt spending weeks alone out on the road with him. But now, it appeared that he had a legitimate reason to be concerned. Catt had never lied to him before. Not that he knew of, at least, and the Catt he knew would never pose for racy pictures, much less send them to anyone. She had already described Jamal as a man with questionable morals and character. Now, it appeared that he was trying to corrupt Catt, but that wasn't going to happen, not as long as Jeremiah Cason had breath in his body.

Jeremiah beckoned Eldon to his office. He knew that he must act quickly and decisively to get his daughter out of Jamal's perilous clutches.

"You wanted to see me?" asked Eldon.

"Yes, come in. Sit down." He offered Eldon a chair. "Have you talked to Catt since she left on this road trip?"

Eldon nodded. "Briefly, right before she left."

"But not since then?"

"No." Eldon was alarmed. "Is something wrong? Have you been able to get in contact with her?"

"Oh, it's nothing like that," Jeremiah assured him. "In fact, I just got off the phone with her a few minutes ago. I am a little concerned about her, though."

"Why?"

Jeremiah leaned back in his chair. "It's this Jamal fellow that she's traveling with. I don't know if I trust him."

"Do you think he might be dangerous?"

"To my daughter's physical well-being, no. But I'm very concerned about his influence on her spiritual and emotion well-being."

"Catt has a good head on her shoulders, sir. She doesn't seem like the type who is easily swayed. She has an excellent spiritual foundation, and I can't see her compromising her standards for anyone."

Jeremiah wasn't as convinced. "Lest we forget, the serpent was craftier than any other animal that the Lord God made. I'm not saying that Catt is naïve or anything like that, but she's away from everything familiar, including her church. It makes it a lot easier to fall."

"So what do you want me to do? You want me to pray for her? Talk to her?"

Jeremiah sighed. "I've got something even better in mind. Don't you have family in D.C.?"

"Yeah, my parents are there. Why?"

Jeremiah drummed his fingers on the desk, plotting. "When is the last time you've been up there to see them?"

Eldon thought back. "Not since Christmas. Their anniversary is coming up. I thought about going up there for the celebration, but I just don't see how I can get away right now."

"If you're worried about time off, don't be. Take as many days as you need."

"Thank you, sir! That's mighty generous of you. But the time off isn't the only issue." He hung his head. "I'm a little strapped for cash right now. Plane tickets don't come cheap these days."

"The Lord always provides a ram, son. You know I'm not a stingy man. If you need help with airfare or anything else, I'll be more than happy to oblige you. God didn't bless me with finances to keep it to myself. He's blessed me, so I can bless you."

Eldon was grateful, but he wasn't stupid. There had to be a catch somewhere. "I'm not one to look a gift horse in the mouth, but you don't even know my parents. Why would you go so far out of your way for them and for me?"

He skimmed through Catt's itinerary. "My daughter should be up that way in a few days. It might be nice if you surprised her. I'm sure she'll be happy to see a familiar face, especially yours."

"Oh, so that's what you meant by having 'something better' in mind?" he concluded, finally catching on.

"I would feel a whole lot better about what's going on up there if I knew Catt had you there to be that spiritual pillar she may need to lean on. Besides, I don't need some smooth-talkin' joker messing with her head only to break her heart once they return and it's back to business as usual. You're the man my daughter needs in her life. I intend to do everything in my power to see to that happening."

"Do you really think this Jamal has ill intentions with Catt?"

"I don't put it past him. And I know my Catt—she's so giving and kind that she might not see his charm and empty promises for what they really are." He cleared his throat to segue into the unspoken truth. "I guess I don't have to tell you that my Catt doesn't get a lot of interest from the opposite sex, not with men being so superficial nowadays. She's liable to fall prey to any man showing her some attention. That's why I like you. You're able to see beyond Catt's physical *issues* and see through to her heart."

"Your daughter is a beautiful woman inside and out to me. I'd never do anything to hurt her," vowed Eldon. "You have my word on that."

Jeremiah stood and patted him affectionately on the back. "Do I also have your word that you'll go to D.C. and show my daughter a good time?"

"I'll do my best."

Jeremiah reached into his pocket and pulled out his wallet. He handed Eldon two crisp one hundred-dollar bills. "This is just a little something to make that happen." Then he slid him a fifty dollar-bill. "Buy your parents something nice on me."

"Thank you, sir!"

"I'll have my secretary book the flight and make all the other arrangements. Your only responsibility is to make my daughter happy and to keep this other fellow as far away from her as possible."

Eldon stuffed the money into his pocket. "Consider it done."

Jeremiah reached for Eldon's hand to shake on it, thus, making it official. The two exchanged knowing smiles.

Between the cash exchange and the handshake and their Cheshire-cat grins, it might appear to the average onlooker that a deal had just been struck with the devil.

Chapter 16

"How much longer do we have?" griped Catt, who was already tired and hungry. She mustered up the energy to smile at a couple walking past their kiosk but not enough to ask them to participate in the promotion.

Jamal checked his watch. "Let's give it another hour or so. I'm pretty beat myself."

Catt closed her eyes and leaned back. "I can't wait to get back to the hotel and take a long hot shower, put on music, and sleep like a bear in winter!"

"That sounds like a plan! You mind if I join you?" asked a male voice other than Jamal's.

Startled, Catt popped her eyes open to see who'd said something to her. She leapt from her chair when she recognized the voice and the face. "Eldon, what a wonderful surprise!" she exclaimed, pulling him into a hug. "What are you doing here?"

He released her from their embrace. "My folks live up here. It's their anniversary. We had a huge party for them last night. When your dad told me you were in town, I was tempted to call and invite you."

"I wish you had. It's so good to see a familiar face." Jamal cleared his throat, not used to being ignored. "Oh . . . Eldon, this is my lab partner, Jamal."

Jamal extended his hand. "What's up, man?"

"God is good, I can't complain. You're not working my girl too hard, are you?" he asked good-naturedly.

Jamal let his eyes drift over Catt's body. "Naw, not yet."

Eldon turned to Catt. "So do you have plans later on tonight? After you finish up here, I mean."

Catt's eyes darted to Jamal, who had now turned his attention to his phone. "What did you have in mind?"

"A nice, somewhat romantic dinner," he answered with a smirk. "You game?"

"Will your parents be joining us?"

"No, the 'newlyweds' have requested a little time to themselves, and I need a good excuse to get out of the house. You don't want to know what kind of sounds I heard coming from their bedroom last night!"

Catt laughed out loud. "I don't think he was hurting her, Eldon."

"I don't intend to stick around long enough to find out who was doing what to whom if I can help it and if you'll join me for dinner."

Before she could reply, Jamal interjected. "Oni's on her way up. I told her we'd meet her for drinks once her plane lands. We'll give her a full debriefing in the morning."

"I'm sorry, I didn't realize you had plans," said Eldon, disappointed.

"I don't," she spat, glaring at Jamal. "Can't you take the meeting with Oni by yourself?"

"It's okay," Eldon assured her. "We can do it some other time."

"No, just join us at the restaurant with Oni. We can get separate tables. That way, we can have dinner and Jamal can have me nearby in case I have to hold his hand and walk him through the meeting."

"I've got something you can hold," mumbled Jamal.

Eldon blinked back and cleared his throat. "Well, on that note, why don't you give me a call when you decide when and where you want to meet, and we'll go from there?"

"Great, I'm looking forward to it."

Eldon gave her another quick hug followed by a kiss on the cheek. "I'll see you tonight." He jetted off in another direction.

Catt sat down, smiling. "Wow, that was a wonderful surprise, wasn't it?"

Jamal shook his head. "He's not your type, you know."

"And just how would you know what my type is?"

"Because I know women. He looks like somebody Daddy picked out for you, Stanley Johnson 2.0."

"Eldon is a good, upstanding Christian man, which is more than I can say for you."

"*Good* and *upstanding* aren't words to describe the kind of man that'll keep a woman from roaming the streets."

"Maybe not the kind of women you deal with. But then again, you know what they call the kind of dogs that like to roam."

"Did I detect a bit of jealousy in that last comment?"

"Why would I be jealous of the skanks you hook up with?"

"I saw how you looked at Yvette that day she came into the lab."

"The look you saw was disgust! What kind of woman shows up to a man's job that early in the morning to tell him where she found her panties?"

"The kind of woman who thoroughly enjoyed losing them the night before," he replied.

She rolled her eyes. "Does everything have to be about sex with you?"

"No, but you can't deny that physical attraction is important."

"I never said it wasn't. I just said it's not the end-all-be-all."

"Are you physically attracted to this Eldon character?"

"Eldon is a very good-looking man, Jamal. Not even you can deny that."

"Yeah, he's a decent-looking brother, I'll give him that. But do you have that chemistry with him? You know, that spark that'll have you sitting at work fantasizing about a joker all day?"

"I don't waste time entertaining sexual fantasies. That's the quickest path to sin. Once you start fixating on stuff like that, it's only a matter of time before you act on it."

"Yeah, that's the whole point," he stated flatly. "Anyway, does he make you feel the way I made you feel that day in the lab?"

Catt's pulse raced. "I don't know what day you're talking about," she lied.

Jamal transfixed her in his gaze. "Yes, you do, Catt. If your conscience let you, you would've ripped my clothes off right then and there!"

"If you're talking about that day—"

He cut her off, posturing himself inches away from her. "I'm talking about that day the heat between us was so crazy that the beakers practically started heating up by themselves! You know *exactly* what day I'm talking about. Now, does this Eldon ever make you feel like that?"

Catt, who was flustered from being so close to him, planted her hands firmly on her hips. "First of all, Eldon would never invade my personal space that way. Furthermore, what Eldon and I have is based on mutual respect and reverence for the Lord, not lust and passion."

"So he doesn't inspire any feelings of a sexual nature whatsoever?"

"No, what we have transcends that."

"Then like I said," Jamal shook his head again, "he ain't the one!"

Chapter 17

Eldon was on his cell phone again. It was the fourth time that a phone call had interrupted his and Catt's dinner. To entertain herself, Catt had taken to guessing which couples in the restaurant were on a first date, which ones were having marital problems, and which men were planning on getting lucky that night.

"Sorry about that," he apologized, pocketing his cell phone. "That was one of the church's parents. She wanted to know if it was sacrilegious to let her son dress up and go trick-or-treating," Eldon replied with a chuckle and adjusted his glasses. "How's your Chicken Marsala?"

Catt nodded politely and dabbed her lips with her napkin. "It's great, really tender."

He reached for her hand. "Catt, I was hoping to talk to you about something tonight."

"Yes," she replied dryly, looking down at her plate instead of at him.

"Well, I wanted to talk about us and the future," he added hopefully.

She lifted her eyes. "What about it?"

"Well, I don't know about you, but the whole dating game isn't really for me. And if you look at the Bible, you never see couples dating. The Lord either sends their mate, or they choose who they want to share a life with and go from there. It's none of this boyfriend-girlfriend, friends-with-benefits stuff you see going on today. I actually think they had the right idea."

Catt stopped eating. "Don't you think it's important for a couple to get to know each other before making a lifetime commitment like marriage?"

"I think it's important that two people share the same values, same ideas about child-rearing, and be equally yoked spiritually. It doesn't take months and years to figure that out, though. You know pretty early on whether you're compatible."

"I suppose so," said Catt, confused by the nature of the conversation. "Where are you going with this?"

"I've been thinking a lot about us and the future. Plus, I've been talking to your dad—" He was interrupted by his phone ringing. "It's Minister Lunsford. I really need to take this call. Do you mind?"

"No, go on. A minister's work is never done, I know."

"Thanks!" He answered the phone. "Good evening, Minister. What can I do for you?"

While Eldon chatted with the minister, Catt turned her head in the direction of a loud but familiar cackle. It was Oni, and although she could only see the back of his head, she already knew who her date was: Jamal.

When Oni spotted Catt looking at them, she waved excitedly. Jamal turned around and, immediately, his eyes locked with hers. Catt's heart began pounding, and Oni signaled for her to join them at their table. Catt excused herself from Eldon, who was still on the phone, and ambled over to them. There was an uncomfortable tension between Catt and Jamal, but Oni seemed not to notice.

"So is this work or play?" asked Catt, noting the half-empty wineglasses on the table.

"Which one does it look like?" Jamal replied snidely.

"I don't know. It almost looks like the two of you are on a date," she remarked. She pasted on a fake smile, but she was still unable to ignore that nagging pinch of jealousy.

"What would be so bad about my taking a beautiful, intelligent woman on a date?" posed Jamal.

"Nothing, I suppose," she lied, not wanting to appear too interested. "It's just that office romance can be a little dicey, that's all."

"Not necessarily," he countered. "I believe in both work and play—all the better if you can kill two birds with one stone."

"I'll drink to that!" agreed Oni, lifting her glass.

"Aren't you worried that people might start to talk?"

Jamal draped his arm around Oni. "Let 'em talk."

Oni dropped the ruse. "He's just yanking your chain, Catt. We're not dating." Oni elbowed him. "Don't mess her like that. You know how seriously Catt takes her work."

"She doesn't let me forget that for a second," said Jamal.

"We've actually been getting a lot accomplished," Oni explained. "Jamal was just showing me the latest figures for the promo. It looks like the two of you have been creating quite the buzz around here. I'm impressed. I think pairing the two of you together was an excellent idea."

Catt begged to differ but kept that thought to herself. "Jamal and I don't always see eye-to-eye on everything, but we're both professional. If you give us a job to do, we're gonna do it."

"I'm glad to hear it. I know you were worried initially, Catt, but I always had a good feeling about the two of you."

Jamal still hadn't taken his arm from around Oni, a move that didn't sit too well with Catt. "Since the two of you are over here working, I might as well join in and shorten the load. I don't mind pulling up a chair," she offered.

"Oh, no," insisted Oni, shooing her away. "We've got this. You go and enjoy your date."

Catt was reluctant to leave. "Are you sure?"

"Yes, we don't mind working all night if we have to," said Jamal. He and Oni exchanged snickers between each other. The sight made Catt cringe. Jamal nodded toward Eldon. "Besides, I think the minister is getting a little lonely over there by himself."

She glanced back at Eldon, who was still on the phone. "I guess I better get back to my date then, huh?"

"I guess you better," he added, gazing at her.

Catt plastered another polite smile across her face and sulked back to her table.

"All right, it'll be on your desk first thing Monday morning. Good-bye." With that, Eldon clasped his phone shut and turned his attention to Catt. "I promise—no more interruptions."

She halfheartedly returned his eager smile. At this point, his yammering on the phone would have been a welcomed relief. It would have left her free to ignore him and to focus all of her attention on Oni and Jamal.

"If you don't mind, I want to continue the conversation we started before the phone rang," said Eldon.

"I'm sorry. I forgot what we were talking about."

"We were talking about how for some couples, it doesn't take months and years of dating to decide you want a future together. Sometimes, the Holy Spirit prompts us to act quicker than that, and I believe that if the Lord has shown you your husband or wife, you shouldn't be afraid to receive that person."

Jamal whispered something in Oni's ear that made her giggle and made Catt wince. "I wonder what they're talking about," she expressed aloud.

"Wonder what who's talking about?"

"Those two." She pointed at Oni and Jamal. She narrowed her eyes to see if she really saw what she thought she was seeing. "Is his hand on her thigh?"

"I can't tell from here. If it is, it'll be a relief to me, though."

She turned around. "Why?"

"I mean, you're out here on the road alone with this guy. I figured he may try to hit on you. It's a relief to know that he's interested in her."

Catt took a sip from her glass. "I can handle my own against Jamal Ford." She looked back at his and Oni's table.

"I know. I just don't like the thought of—"

"His hand is *definitely* on her thigh!" blurted out Catt. "They might as well have sex right there on the table!" Embarrassed by the outburst, which was heard by more than a few people, she excused herself to go to the restroom.

She scolded herself in the mirror. "Catt Cason, get it together!" She shook off the feelings of jealousy that had been eating away at her all night long, and refreshed her lipstick. The least she should do for Eldon is return to the table looking flawless.

"Aha, I caught you!" ribbed Oni, joining her in the mirror. "I see you trying to get all sexy for that tall drink of water you came in here with."

Catt was less-than-thrilled by Oni's presence. "Oh, hey. I didn't hear you come in."

"I'm not surprised. You were a million miles away just now. I hope you're not in here thinking about work when your date clearly has other things on his mind. Jamal told me that he came up from Charlotte just to see you. He must be very special or must think you are."

"Seeing me was pretty much an after-thought. Eldon really came to town for his parents' anniversary."

Oni set her purse down near the sink to reapply her makeup. "So do the two of you have big plans for tonight?"

"We're sort of playing it by ear." She paused. "What about you and Jamal?"

Oni fiddled with her hair. "There's no telling what that man has up his sleeves, but I'm sure going to enjoy finding out!"

"So it *is* more than just work between you two," insinuated Catt.

Oni took note of Catt's curt tone. "You wouldn't have a problem with that, would you, Catt?"

Catt shrugged off the question dismissively. "Why would I? You're both consenting adults."

"I don't know, it's just a vibe I picked up."

Catt feigned indifference. "What you and Jamal do outside of the office is none of my business."

Oni reached for her purse. "I guess I'll see you tomorrow. Enjoy your evening." She headed toward the door.

"It's just weird, that's all," spoke up Catt.

Oni turned and faced her. "What's weird?"

"You dating Jamal. He doesn't really seem like your type."

"Let me see . . . attractive, smart, driven—that's *exactly* my type."

Catt inched toward her. "Yeah, but he doesn't strike me as the kind who's looking to settle down."

"Even better—neither am I."

"And he's a notorious flirt," she added. "I mean, I can't tell you how many times I've seen him hitting on women around the office."

"He's assertive and knows what he wants. I like that." Oni raised an eyebrow. "Honestly, I didn't know you cared so much about who I dated. You've never been this vocal about it before."

"Well, we're friends, right?" covered Catt with a saccharine smile.

Oni nodded but wasn't buying. "I hope that's all it is."

"Of course, it is. I just don't want to see my friend get hurt."

"I appreciate your concern, Catt." Oni crossed her arms in front of her. "But if I didn't know better, I might think you were a little jealous."

"Me? Jealous of you and Jamal?" She forced a laugh. "I just find it odd that he's seeing you at nights and spending his days kissing me."

Oni blinked. "He kissed you?"

"He tried to, but I pushed him off," revealed Catt. She hadn't planned on telling her what happened, but her jealousy had taken on a voice and a life of its own.

"Next time you ought to go for it," urged Oni. "He's a great kisser." She looked down at her watch. "I better get out of here. Don't keep Eldon waiting."

"I won't," she said unenthusiastically. "Have fun."

Oni looked back at her as she sauntered out. "We intend to."

Catt quickly called on the Lord to forgive her for all of the unspeakable names she was lacerating Oni with in her mind. She took a deep breath and walked out to meet Eldon.

"I thought you fell in," joked Eldon, standing up to pull out Catt's chair for her. "You were gone a long time."

She sat down. "I ran into my boss. We exchanged a little girl talk."

"Did you get the lowdown on her and your lab partner?"

"Not really, we mostly talked about work." She asked God for forgiveness again for lying.

"Those two looked kind of cozy," Eldon observed, diving into his grilled salmon. Catt glanced at the two of them over her shoulder just as Jamal took Oni's hand into his to lift her out of her seat.

Stewing inside, Catt watched them walk away. "That's Jamal Ford for you—always on the prowl. He's so arrogant and pretentious. I don't know what Oni sees in him. He is so smug and full of himself!" she spewed.

"Whoa, you don't have to get so worked up. You don't like the guy—I get it." Eldon shook his head and continued eating.

But you don't get it, thought Catt. Not only did she *not* hate Jamal, but it was becoming clear to her she was incredibly attracted to him. It was an emotion that was better off remaining repressed.

"Let's order some drinks!" suggested Catt, suddenly enthused and very willing to numb her emotions with alcohol.

"We have tea right here."

"I don't want that kind of tea. I'm thinking the Long Island variety."

"Sister Cason, I don't know if that's such a good idea," voiced Eldon, reverting back to his ministerial mode. "In fact, I didn't even know you drank."

She raised a finger to summon their waiter's attention. "I usually don't, but tonight, I don't feel like doing the usual."

"I think it's important we keep a clear head. You never know when we may be called upon to minister for the Lord."

"Fine, you can be the designated witness. I'm having a drink!"

Three Long Island Iced Teas later, Catt's head was spinning and she was drunk.

"Catt, we should really get out of here. You need to sleep this off. Your father would kill me if he knew I watched you sit here and down three drinks."

It was becoming difficult for her to fully process what Eldon was saying, partially from the alcohol but mostly from being bombarded with thoughts of Oni and Jamal.

"Maybe you're right, Eldon," she agreed, then belched loudly. "I've been a very, very bad girl. Daddy wouldn't like that."

"No, he wouldn't!" Eldon was tense and nervous as he signed the receipt for their dinner bill. He slipped his credit card back into his wallet.

She giggled. "But I bet I know who does like bad girls."

Eldon shook his head and helped her out of her chair and out of the restaurant.

"Hey, wake up," said Eldon, rousing Catt from a near-stupor as the cab dropped them off in front of Catt's hotel.

Catt slumped down in the seat. "Just let me rest five more minutes."

"Here, lean on my arm," instructed Eldon as she staggered out of the car. He dragged her to the elevator and onto the floor of her hotel room, as she was too inebriated to walk unassisted.

"Eldon, you're such a great guy, you know that?" she slurred, rubbing his face.

"And you're a very drunk girl, did you know that?" Eldon was right: she was drunk but not drunk enough to erase the memory of her body clinging to Jamal's or the thrill of having his lips, soft and moist, brushing across her skin that day in the lab.

Eldon finagled the key card out of her hand and unlocked the door. "Watch your step." He flipped the light switch and ushered her inside.

Catt smiled and wrapped her arms around his neck. "Let's do something crazy! Let's make love right here, right now."

He disengaged himself from her. "Catt, you're drunk. Once I get you settled in, I'm going back to my parents' house alone."

"But why?" she whined, nearly toppling over.

Eldon sighed. "Catt, this isn't like you. You're one of the most levelheaded and responsible women I know. What's gotten into you?"

"I want *you* to get into me," she purred, seizing him by the waist. "Come on, Eldon. I know I'm a big girl, but don't you think I'm sexy?"

He rebuffed her again. "I think you're very sexy . . . when you're sober!"

She pulled out her cell phone. "You wanna see sexy? Let me show you some of my pictures . . ."

Eldon snatched the phone out of her hand and set it down. "Catt, you don't know what you're saying. No doubt you're going to burst an appendix when you wake up in the morning and realize that you were in this hotel room, drunk and making a fool of yourself."

She stumbled back a few steps. "Making a fool of myself," she echoed bitterly. "What you mean by that?"

"The woman you are right now is not the kind of woman I need at my side, helping me build our ministry and the Faith Temple name. I thought that we were two-of-a-kind, you know—driven, ambitious, passionate about the Lord's work. That's what attracted me to you. But this isn't you, not the *you* I thought I knew anyway."

She kicked off her shoes. "Yeah, you like boring me. Boring scripture-quoting, Sunday dinner-eating, always-doing-the-right-thing me. That's the only Catt you and my father want me to be."

Eldon sat her down on the bed. "We want you to be the virtuous woman of God that you are, not . . . *this*. I can't help but think that it's Jamal Ford's negative influence that's got you acting this way."

"Jamal's been showing me how to live. There's more to life than Faith Temple, you know."

"Yeah, I know." Eldon pulled back the duvet for Catt to crawl underneath. "You're going to be my first lady one day. I can't have you getting drunk and taking phone pictures when that time comes, you got it?"

Catt nodded and lay down, already half asleep. "I got it—no drinking, no pictures."

"And no Jamal Ford either!" stipulated Eldon and switched off her light. He waited for Catt to reply, but she had drifted off to sleep.

Eldon hadn't anticipated opposition from another man in his quest to win Catt's affections and his rightful place as Faith Temple's senior pastor, but Jamal Ford was proving to be someone to be watched and, if necessary, eliminated.

Chapter 18

"Hold up—I'm coming!" called Jamal, racing to catch the elevator. Catt begrudgingly held the door open for him. She studied his face, searching for something that would give her a clue as to what happened between him and Oni the night before.

"Did you get Oni's text about meeting her across the street for breakfast this morning?" she asked him.

"She told me about it last night."

"I bet she did," mumbled Catt.

"Why do you look so mad this morning?"

"Who said anything about being mad?"

Jamal smiled. "Cheer up. The birds are singing, it's a beautiful day . . ."

"I guess I don't have to ask what *you* did last night," she grumbled as they entered the hotel's lobby.

"No thanks to you. Oni told me about your little outburst in the ladies' room yesterday."

"I just thought she should know what she was getting into."

"Funny—I kind of thought you were blocking."

"Why would I need to do that? Didn't you notice that I had a date too?"

He chuckled. "You mean that simp you were with last night?"

"Watch it—that *simp* is an anointed man of God."

Jamal moved in closer. "Yeah, I watched you last night. You seemed to have a great time watching him yapping on the phone all night."

"You mean you stopped drooling over Oni long enough to look at me?"

A smile creased his face. "So, *that's* what this is about? You're jealous."

"No, I'm not!" she insisted. "I just think that it's in very poor taste to be hitting on your boss. We're supposed to be professionals."

"It drives you crazy, doesn't it? You probably spent the whole night visualizing me kissing her, putting that tingle in her spine."

"You're a pig," she shot back. "I really thought Oni had better taste than this."

"Will you chill out? The only ride I gave Oni last night was the one back to her hotel room after dinner, so you can put your claws back in."

"What you and Oni do or don't do is of no interest to me."

"I'm glad to hear it because we're going out again next time she meets up with us."

Catt was stunned. "Oni agreed to a go out with you again? I suppose we're all entitled to mistakes every now and then."

"Obviously, I'm one mistake she doesn't mind repeating."

"Are the two of you an official couple now?"

"No." He grazed her with his eyes. "I'm interested in someone else."

"How *do* you keep track of them all?" She shook her head. "I suppose that little things like AIDS and unwanted pregnancies mean absolutely nothing to you."

"I always handle my business when it comes to that."

"Says you!" challenged Catt. "You probably have babies and baby mamas running all over the country and don't even know it."

He was quiet for a moment, almost somber. "I don't have any children in the United States or anywhere else in the world."

"How can you be so sure with the way you slide in and out of anything in a skirt?"

"I don't have any children," he repeated. "Life is precious to me, especially a child's life. Don't ever say that again." He charged ahead of her, letting the hotel's front door close behind him and in her face.

"What was that about?" she demanded, following closely behind him.

"You talk too much, and most of the time, you don't have a clue about what you're talking about," barked Jamal.

"Since when have you been unable to take a joke?"

"Just drop it, Catt."

"Jamal, if I struck a nerve with something I said, I'm sorry," she added with sincerity.

"I thought I told you to drop it."

"I didn't mean to say anything to hurt you."

He stopped and turned around. "You didn't hurt me, Catt. In order to hurt me, I'd have to care about you, and, frankly, you're just not that important to me." Jamal darted across the street without so much as looking back to see her reaction.

Catt didn't have any delusions about his feelings for her, nor did she take his flirting as anything more than just his way with women. But having it confirmed hurt Catt more than she ever expected it would.

Chapter 19

As Catt was setting up her workstation following their meeting with Oni, Jamal sneaked up from behind her, grabbing her at the waist, and kissed her on the cheek.

She didn't return his playful mood. "Jamal, don't..."

"Why not?"

She pushed him away. "Because you were very mean to me earlier today."

"I was having a bad day. Are you going to hold that against me?"

"Yes. Having a bad day is no excuse to terrorize other people."

"You're too anal, Catt. I was upset at the time. You know I didn't mean all that crap about not caring about you."

"How am I supposed to know that?" she demanded.

"Because you know me. Anyway, you're gonna want to forgive me when you find out what I just copped..."

"You bought me diamonds?" joked Catt. "You really know how to get back into a girl's good graces!"

"Yeah, there's a diamond involved, but not the kind you mean," he hedged. "I got us tickets for the baseball game tonight. You haven't seen a game until you've seen one in Wrigley Field."

"Sounds like fun. You know, I think I actually have tickets to that game already."

"How did you get tickets? It's sold out."

She brushed him off. "It's a long story."

"So does this mean I'm forgiven," ventured Jamal.

She smacked her lips. "Only because I like baseball."

After giving Telegenic a full day's work and then some, Catt and Jamal were ready to kick back and enjoy the game.

"So much for eating healthy," replied Jamal as they walked back from the concession stand cradling an armload of drinks, hot dogs, and popcorn.

"It's a game!" argued Catt. "You're allowed to pig out and have fun."

"I didn't think you knew how to do that."

"What, pig out? Have you seen these hips?"

"No, I didn't think you knew how to have fun."

"Keep on and I'll leave you in the nosebleed section," threatened Catt.

"Oh, my seats ain't good enough?" chided Jamal.

She led him down near the front. "I didn't say that. I just think we might be able to see better from *my* seats."

"Catt, where exactly are your seats?" Jamal asked cautiously as they made their way past the cheap seats into the pricier ones.

"Right down here—excuse me," she said scooting past other spectators to make her way to the front rows where the players' families and guests sat.

Jamal refused to budge. "Catt, we can't sit here! You're gonna get us thrown out!"

She pulled him along. "Will you relax—sheesh! Do you think I'm crazy enough to sit down in someone else's seats?"

"Catt, are these *seriously* your seats?" asked a bewildered Jamal, reluctant to sit down.

"Of course, they are," she answered casually, digging into the popcorn.

"How? Why?"

"Suffice it to say, I'm cool with one of the players."

"You know one of the players?" asked Jamal in awe. "Which one?"

She leaned over and pointed. "You see the cutie playing shortstop? His family is from Charlotte. He grew up in the church. He's a real good friend of the family, sends us tickets all the time."

He raised an eyebrow. "Friend of the family, huh? How *good* of a friend is he to you?"

She blushed. "What do you mean?"

Jamal pointed at her. "Yeah, I know that look. Baseballs aren't the only thing that number ten's been hittin'!"

"It's nothing like that," denied Catt, laughing.

"Don't play innocent with me, Catt. I'm sure you took your nose out of the Bible long enough to notice a fairly decent-looking guy with a lot of money and 'pro ball player' on his résumé. What went on between the two of y'all?"

Catt yielded. "Okay, I admit we hung out a couple of times, but it was nothing serious, just a high school thing."

"And *that's* it?" pushed Jamal.

"What's up with all the questions, Jamal? Are you jealous?"

"Go on somewhere with that, girl," Jamal sneered, brushing off her question. He paused for a moment, then continued his line of questioning. "So, what—he used to be your man or something?"

"No." Catt tuned back into the game. "That was too high! Can you believe he swung at that? What are you thinking?" she heckled to the player at bat.

"But I bet he's the one who took you to Belize, right?"

"What?" She diverted her attention from the game to him. "And why am I being interrogated?"

"I'm just saying, if a man is taking you on trips—"

"*He was safe!*" yelled Catt along with the rest of the crowd over the bad call by the referees.

"Catt, are you listening to me?"

"Did you see that?" she ranted. "He touched the base right before that guy tagged him. He was safe!"

"Catt, can you focus for five minutes?"

"I *am* focused! I saw him touch the base. He was safe."

"I'm not talking about that. I'm talking about this friend of yours."

"Number ten? What about him?"

"Do you like him?"

She shrugged. "Sure, we're friends."

"Well, are you friends with him like you're friends with me?"

"Yes."

"Have you ever slept with him?" pried Jamal.

"Now who's being nosey?"

Jamal continued to sulk as Catt enjoyed the game. At one point when the White Sox were in the field, Catt smiled and waved as number ten darted onto the outfield.

"You know he can't see you," needled Jamal.

"Give it a rest, Jamal."

"Is he going to come charging up here if he sees me with his woman?"

She taunted him. "You scared?"

"Scared of what?"

Catt looked at Jamal and shook her head.

During the seventh inning, a home-run ball careened into the stands near where they were sitting. After a mad scramble by other fans to secure the ball, Catt leapt with the grace and precision of a ballerina and caught the ball in midair. The crowd went into a frenzied cheer for both the home run and the catch, which was caught by the JumboTron.

"Where did you learn to do that?" asked Jamal stunned.

"Are you kidding? I was the best first-base player my softball team in high school ever had!" Jamal was still floored. "You thought a big girl couldn't jump?"

"I don't know what to think anymore when it comes to you," he admitted.

"You can never assume, Jamal. You know what they say about people who do that."

He shook his head and laughed. "You're just full of surprises, aren't you, girl? I can't wait to see your next trick."

Catt winked an eye. "Watch, wait, and be amazed!"

Chapter 20

Jamal yawned and tried to shake himself awake and focused, but he was so sleepy that the dividing lines in the road seemed to be running together. "I can barely keep my eyes opened."

"I told you not to try to get on the road after the game," lectured Catt, who was nodding off herself. "How much longer 'til we get to Cleveland?"

Jamal checked the navigation system. "Four hours," he groaned. "I can't even do it, Catt. You're gonna have to drive."

"I'm just as sleepy as you are!" she cried. "We put in the same time at work and the same three hours at the game."

"You never drive!" complained Jamal. "This ain't gon' work. Either you're gonna drive, or I'm stopping to get a room for the night."

"We're in the middle of nowhere," Catt pointed out, looking ahead at the dark, deserted road. "This is the kind of place where the police usually find the body years later."

"Well, Catt, if they kill me, at least I'll be able to get some sleep!"

They drove another ten miles before Jamal spotted Sunlight Inn, a cheap one-story motel, probably more accustomed to being the site for illicit affairs more than a good night's sleep.

"We're checkin' in," asserted Jamal, pulling off the road to the motel's parking lot.

"Jamal, will you look at that place? It's got STD written all over it! Let's just ride a little further down the road."

Jamal stretched his seat back. "Catt, if I could go further, I would, but this is it. I don't even have the strength to get out and pay for the room." He passed her his credit card. "Go and handle that."

"It's almost three o'clock in the morning. I'm not getting out this car to check in some dingy motel. No!"

Jamal let his eyes fall shut. "Put all that praying you do to good use. The Lord will protect you."

Seeing that she was out of options, Catt called for a legion of angels to camp out around her as she made her way from the car to the lobby—if it could be called such—of the motel.

The door was locked. She rang the bell and was greeted by a smarmy, chain-smoking desk clerk, who talked to her through an armhole in the window.

"You want a room?" he droned.

"Yes, sir, two please."

He fired off several hacking coughs. Suddenly, Catt was grateful for the plastic window that stood between them. "That'll be $33.76 a piece."

She handed him the credit card. "Umm . . . can I request your best room or at least your cleanest one?"

He tossed two keys attached to green rubber "Sunlight Inn" key chains through the hole. Slowly, he blew out a ring of smoke. "They're all clean. Rooms 123 and 124, 'round the corner to your left."

When Catt returned to the car, Jamal was already asleep. She poked him to get his attention. "If you were hoping for room service and a mint on the pillow, you might be outta luck." She tossed him a room key.

"At this point, I'll settle for a blanket and a pillow."

"I'm glad *clean* is optional, considering where we are."

Jamal mustered the energy to drive around the corner to their rooms. He walked Catt to her door.

She unlocked it and flipped the light switch. The lamp cast a dim light on the two full-sized beds, dusty dresser, and watercolor art that made up the room. "Maybe I should've left the light off," she mumbled, looking around at the sad excuse of a motel.

Jamal turned up his nose. "That wouldn't have done anything about the smell," he noted. The room reeked of curry chicken and stale beer. "Looks like they spared *all* expenses with this one!"

Catt pressed down on the bed's flowery comforter to make sure the bed was sturdy. "As a rule of thumb, I never stay at a hotel where I can get into my room from the outside. Nothing about this place looks safe . . . or sanitary, for that matter."

"Are you going to be okay over here by yourself?"

"It's just for one night, right? I'm sure I've stayed in worse places." She frowned at spotting a dead roach near the bed. "Then again, maybe not."

"You know, this doesn't look like the safest neighborhood. Maybe you should crash with me for the night. The rooms do have two beds."

"Are you sure?" The prospect of spending the night with Jamal appealed to her about as much as spending the night alone in the room. She pulled back the comforter and found a condom wrapper underneath.

"You need more proof?"

Catt frowned in disgust. "Jamal, this place is beyond gross! Let's just go somewhere else."

"Let's check out my room first. It might be better."

"It would have to work hard to be worse," she quipped.

Jamal unlocked his door. Absent from his room were the roaches, condoms, and lingering odors. "Okay, it's not so bad," he replied, scanning the room for rodents and bugs.

Catt pulled back the sheets on one of the beds. "It doesn't appear that anyone's had sex in this bed within the last twenty-four hours."

Jamal sat down on the bed and pulled off his shoes. "See? I told you it wasn't so bad."

"I'm still getting my disinfectant spray out of the car and hosing this place down. I'm getting the blankets out of the trunk too. There's no way I'm letting these sheets touch my skin!"

True to her word, Catt used an entire can of disinfectant spraying down the sheets, the toilet, the doorknobs, and the sink. She flared her blanket out over the bed and lay down to rest, only to find that all of the cleaning and spraying had taken the tiredness out of her.

If she was going to be up, she needed company. "Psst, are you asleep?"

Jamal turned over in his bed. "Would it matter if I said yes?"

"I can't sleep," she told him.

He yawned. "Well, I can! Good night!"

"Don't you want to talk?"

"Not at three in the morning, no."

"Is this the kind of place you take your women to when you want to remember the sex but not her name?"

"I told you I'm trying to get some sleep, Tonya," he groaned.

"Tonya?" repeated Catt. "Who's that?"

"What are you talking about?"

"You called me Tonya."

"I called you Catt."

"No, you called me Tonya," insisted Catt.

"Okay, so I called you Tonya. It was a Freudian slip."
Catt sat up. "So who's Tonya?"

"Just some chick. Now can you please shut up so I
can get some sleep?"

"I will as soon as you tell me about Tonya."

Jamal pulled the blankets around him. "Let's see . . .
we met, it didn't work out; now it's over. End of conversation."

"Jamal—" she broke in.

"Why are we even talking about this, especially when
I can think of a much better use for that mouth of yours
at this time of night?"

She hurled a pillow at him. "Tell me what brought
you to Charlotte."

"Work—you already know that. Now chill out with
all the questions and go to sleep."

Catt proceeded with her questions as if she didn't
hear him. "I don't get it. You're a brilliant chemist who
could get a job anywhere. Why would you settle for a
company like Telegenic? There's got to be more to the
story."

"I've always liked North Carolina."

"So you *are* from North Carolina?"

"Yes. I spent the first part of my life in Raleigh."

"Really?"

"Yes, really!" he replied, exasperated. "You've asked
enough questions for one night. I need some rest."

"Just one more question, I promise."

"What is it?"

"What happened that made you think that you had
to go all the way to Paris to get away from it?"

"I was ready for a change."

She crossed her arms over her chest. "I don't believe you. I think it's more than that, and I think it has something to do with Tonya."

"You think too much. The best remedy for that is a good night's sleep."

"Come on, Jamal, there's nobody here but the two of us. You can trust me. I want to know about Tonya and the reason you left all those years ago."

"If I tell you, will you promise to shut up?"

She held up her right hand. "Scout's honor."

He paused and sighed. "Tonya taught me rule number one—never fall in love."

"How so?"

Jamal sat up, rubbing his eyes. "When I met her, I was young and still stupid enough to believe that love could conquer all."

"Some of us still believe," she added.

"You can save yourself a lot of trouble and therapy by forgetting that now."

"She broke your heart, didn't she?" surmised Catt.

"Not in the way you mean. Tonya and I were married. She's the only woman I've ever gotten on my knees to ask for anything."

"You never told me that you'd been married before. Honestly, I didn't see you as the marrying kind."

"Well, I was. We were married for about six years."

"What happened?"

He lay back down. "I really don't want to talk about this right now."

"Sometimes it helps to talk about things that have hurt you."

"All the talking in the world won't change a thing. Nothing I do will ever bring her back."

Catt sighed in empathy. "You must have really loved her."

He nodded. "I did. Kennedy was my whole world."

"Kennedy?" She frowned, confused. "I thought her name was Tonya."

"Kennedy is . . ." he swallowed hard. "Kennedy was our little girl."

"Little girl?" she echoed. This was the first time Jamal had ever made reference to having a child. Catt paused, building the courage to ask. "You said *was* your little girl. Did she . . . I mean, is she . . ."

"She's dead, Catt," filled in Jamal. "She was only four years old."

Catt flung her hand over her mouth. "My God, you must have been devastated."

"It's true, you know. You never get over losing a child." A sad smile spread across his face. "I can still hear her now saying, 'Daddy, look what I found!' She was so beautiful too. She had my complexion, but she was Tonya up and down. Kennedy was a bright little thing too—always asking questions and wanting to know how things worked. If she hadn't had that asthma attack . . ." He lowered his head. He didn't say anything, but Catt knew that he was crying to himself.

She gave him a few minutes to compose himself before going on. Now, his brusque reaction to her making jokes about having children all over the country made sense to her. "I know going through that kind of heartbreak must've been hell for you and your wife. At least you had each other to lean on."

Jamal shook his head. "Ironically, that's the very thing that broke us apart. The pain of Kennedy's death was just too much."

"I've heard that the death of a child can destroy even the strongest marriage."

"We didn't know how to be there for each other, I guess. I tried, but Tonya felt like I was 'smothering' her, as she put it. She never really accepted that Kennedy was gone, never wanted to talk about it. She completely lost it when I suggested that we pack up Kennedy's things and donate them to charity. She wanted to leave her room and everything just like it was before she died, but I couldn't live in the past like that. It was like having to relive her death every day. After that, things between us went from bad to worse. Eventually, we stopped talking, stopped trying to make it work. I guess losing Kennedy was something we couldn't fight against, no matter how much we loved each other."

Catt's heart broke for him. "I'm so sorry this happened to you, Jamal."

"Don't be. I stopped being hurt over the marriage a long time ago. Losing Kennedy is going to always be with me."

"Is that when you left for Paris?"

"There was nothing left for me here except memories. My little girl was gone, my marriage was over—I just needed a fresh start."

"But don't you see what you've done instead? You don't let anyone get close to you. Jamal, that's no way to live."

"This's how I like it—no strings. Nobody gets too close, and nobody gets hurt."

"You could have so much more than that. The God I serve is so much bigger than anything you've had to go through, even the death of your little girl."

"God and I don't really see eye-to-eye these days," he admitted. "After watching my child fight for each breath, then die, everything changed for me. I mean, I know there's a God, but I'm not so sure He knows there's a Jamal Ford."

"Of course He does! Without God, we have nothing, Jamal. You can't turn your back on the one person who can help you no matter what."

"He turned His back on me first. I know that God works for some people. I don't happen to be one of those people. After losing my wife and my child, money and sex became the saving grace that I once believed the Lord to be," he confessed. "Whatever desire I had to believe, love, or be loved was burned out by heartbreak and disappointment and was replaced with ambition and a string of one-night stands."

"He's still there for you, Jamal. God never turns His back on us. In His Word, He says, 'I'll never leave you nor forsake you.' You've got to trust in that; trust in Him."

"He took my child away from me. How am I supposed to put my trust in a God who'd do that?"

"God didn't take her. Furthermore, Kennedy probably knows more about God now than any of us down here on earth will ever know. Heaven's not a bad place to be, Jamal."

He shook his head. "All this talk about heaven and God ain't doing me a bit of good here on earth," he stated bitterly. "Kennedy is gone, and she was my reason for living."

"God should be your reason," Catt informed him. "We can't make idols out of people, not even our children. Another person can't fill the place in your heart where God is supposed to be. He's the only one big enough to fill it."

Jamal turned over in his bed. "You have your beliefs, Catt, and I have mine."

"Jamal, we need to talk about this some more," pushed Catt.

"No, *you* need to talk about this some more. *I* need to get some sleep."

Catt gave up and turned off the lamp. The conversation was dead for now, but she had every intention of a resurrection before the week was out.

***

Catt was awakened from her sleep by Jamal crying out in his sleep and thrashing about in bed. His machinations were enough to set her heart racing in fear.

She rushed to his side to rouse him. "Jamal, wake up!"

Jamal gasped and sat up in the bed. He looked around frantically, briefly not remembering where he was.

"Are you okay? You're sweating," she said, wiping his forehead. "You were talking and tossing in your sleep. You scared me."

He broke away from her and stood up. "I'm all right," he said, trying to catch his breath.

"Wow, that must've been some dream!" she exclaimed. "Do you want to talk about it?"

"What for?" he asked gruffly. "It was just a dream."

"I heard you call out to your father," whispered Catt. "Is there something going on with you and him?"

Jamal grabbed his shirt, which was hanging from the back of a chair. "I'm going out."

"At this hour?"

"At any hour I want to. I'm a grown man."

"Jamal, I can tell something is bothering you. Maybe it would help to pray . . ."

He stepped into his shoes. "Praying is your thing, not mine."

"Then I'll pray for you. Just don't go."

"I need to get out of the room. It feels like I'm suffocating." He snatched his room key from the dresser and marched toward the door.

"Jamal, wait," cried Catt. "Whatever it is that's bothering you, God can lift that burden. Turn it over to Him. He'll see you through."

Jamal opened the door. "Tell God thanks but no thanks. I've seen what He can do. I'm better off taking care of myself."

Chapter 21

Catt covered her head with her pillow and tried to ignore the door knocking that had stirred her out of a deep sleep.

After spending a rough night at the Sunlight Inn, driving four hours that morning, and spending all day working, she was exhausted. She and Jamal both agreed that they deserved to splurge on an upscale hotel and to take the next day off.

"Go away!" she moaned, rolling over. She had already settled into bed for the night and had no intentions of getting up before noon. The knocking continued. "Go away!" she called louder. Now the person began pounding on the door.

She unwillingly threw off her blankets and dragged herself to the door to see who it was. Peering through the peephole she saw Jamal waving at the little hole in the door.

Catt unlocked and opened the door. "Jamal, what are you doing here?" she asked, yawning.

"You look like hell," he observed.

"Really?" she replied dryly. "That's better than I thought."

"Come on," he said, beckoning her with his finger.

She noticed that he was wearing a sweat suit and clutching a basketball. "Do you know what time it is? Shouldn't you be in your own hotel room asleep?"

"I couldn't sleep. I kept thinking about you saying that you sucked at basketball, so I decided that it was time that you didn't suck at it anymore."

"Jamal, it's almost one o'clock in the morning. I don't think I've had more than three hours of sleep in the past forty-eight hours. I'm sleepy, it's cold out here, and I'm going to bed. Good night."

She proceeded to shut the door, but Jamal propped it back open. "Not tonight! Come on—grab your sneaks and your game face. Let's go." He made his way inside the hotel room.

"Jamal, I'm tired," whined Catt.

"So was I when you tried to talk my head off last night."

"Did you have another nightmare?" she asked, suspecting that might be the reason he couldn't sleep.

"You ask too many questions."

Catt was too tired to pursue it any further. "Just come back in the morning." She lay down on the sofa and began dozing off again.

"It *is* morning." Jamal rummaged through her suitcase and pulled out a navy blue hooded sweat shirt and pants.

"Here." He nudged her to wake her up. Catt groaned in protest. "All right, then, you just sit there, and I'll do all of the work." He crouched down and slid the pant legs over her feet. "I always thought I'd be taking your clothes off, not putting them on," he mentioned, lifting her by the waist to pull the pants over her hips and pajama shorts. "You can keep your T-shirt on. We'll just put this on over it." He put the shirt over her head and pulled her arms through the sleeves. He then slid socks over her feet and tied her shoes. "Okay, you're set now—come on."

Catt grudgingly stood up but instead of walking toward the door, she turned in the direction of her bed.

"Wrong way," said Jamal, grabbing her and ushering her toward the door. "Here, hold this." He secured the basketball under her arm. She was still half-asleep when he led her out the door.

"I think we should start with shooting. That's probably where you're having the most trouble," said Jamal as he dribbled the ball down the court, which was illuminated by light posts and the full moon. They were at a vacated basketball court near their hotel that they'd driven to.

"Are you ready?" he asked eagerly. She yawned and stood akimbo. He passed the ball to her. She let it drop at her feet.

"You're not even trying, Catt. I know you're not that sleepy." He picked up the ball and tossed it to her again. This time she caught it.

"Good, you're waking up. Now let me see you shoot." She made a paltry attempt at shooting the ball. It stopped several feet short of the goal.

Jamal retrieved the ball. "Your handling is all wrong," he noted. "Look, you hold the ball like this and kind of bend your knees this way," he said, demonstrating. "Then let go." He flung the ball and sank it into the hoop. "Here, you try," he instructed after getting the ball back.

Catt tried to emulate what Jamal had done, but the ball wound up behind the backboard. "This is stupid," she complained.

Jamal clapped his hands to encourage her. "Okay, that was better. Try again."

She made another attempt. This time, the ball ricocheted off of the rim and to the gravel. Catt smacked her lips in disapproval. "Jamal, I told you I can't do it. I'm no good at this. If I haven't learned in thirty-one years, I'm not going to learn in one night."

"Stop being so down on yourself. You almost got it. Let me help you a little." He positioned himself behind her to assist her. He was close enough to smell her shampoo and feel the heat from her warm body. Her behind was pressing against his groin, and, for a moment, basketball was the furthest thing from his mind.

"Don't get ideas back there!" she warned with a laugh. "Come on, let's do this." With his hand cupped around hers, they tossed the ball. It bounced off the backboard but didn't go into the basket.

"Dang it!" screeched Catt, frustrated. She jogged to retrieve the ball. She resumed her position and aimed the ball carefully.

"Bend your knees a little," he coached. She obeyed and threw the ball. It swirled into the basket. She squealed gleefully.

"That's it!" praised Jamal. On impulse, he outstretched his arms to her to give her a congratulatory hug, and she happily slid into his embrace. They exchanged awkward glances afterward. Catt broke the tension by attempting another shot. She missed but sank the three following that.

"All right, Miss WNBA, let's try a half-court shot." They moved a few feet down the court. Catt shot and narrowly missed. They both winced. Jamal seemed to be as disappointed as she was.

"Try one more time," he urged. That time, she made it. In their excitement, they ended up back in each other's arms.

"Maybe we should go back to the hotel," suggested Jamal.

Catt released herself from his grip. "Are you kidding? I'm on fire now!" She took another shot.

"All right," said Jamal, forcibly shaking himself from his amorous mood. "How about a little twenty-one?" He stole possession of the ball from her, and she attempted to block his shot, which toppled into the basket.

"You're no match for me, girl," he taunted, dribbling the ball around her. He ventured a layup, which missed and was rebounded by Catt. She jumped up to make the shot but came down hard on her foot. It twisted beneath the weight of her body. She cried out in pain and fell to the ground.

Jamal raced to her side. "Are you all right?"

"It hurts," she groaned while trying to massage the foot.

Jamal examined her foot and ankle. "You probably just sprained it a little. You'll live, though. Come on, let's get you back to the room and off of this foot." He helped her up and held her by the waist for support as she limped back to the car.

When they reached her hotel room, he helped her ease down on the couch and propped her foot up on the sofa pillows.

"You stay here for a minute. I'll be right back," he ordered. He disappeared into the bathroom while Catt continued to nurse her injured foot. Some minutes later, he returned.

"What were you doing back there?" she asked. "And I don't recall giving you free reign of my room either. You can do your business across the hall in your bathroom."

He smiled mischievously. "Just shut up and take off your clothes."

"Do what?" she balked. "Here I am over here in excruciating pain because you decided that you wanted to play basketball at one o'clock in the morning, and you have the audacity to try to turn this into some kind of seduction! You're sick, Jamal; please leave!"

"Why would I try to seduce you now?" he asked, kneeling down beside her. "If that was the case, I would have done it when I had you half-naked and asleep."

She immediately tensed up. "Don't joke like that!" she said gravely.

"I was kidding, Catt."

"Just don't play like that!" she reiterated. She still looked upset.

He cocked his head to the side. "Are you okay?"

"Yes," she replied angrily, then calmed down. "I'm all right. I know someone who that actually happened to, and there was nothing funny about it." She changed the subject. "Now, you never did answer my question about what you were doing back there."

"How about I show you instead?" He swept her off of the couch and shooed her down the hallway. True to form, she protested the entire way. Jamal ignored her and opened the door to the bathroom.

Catt was speechless once they entered. Jamal had drawn a bubble bath and had lit the complimentary candles from their posh hotel room around the garden tub. The aroma of lavender and chamomile radiated from the candles and lingered in the room.

"What's all this?" she asked stunned. He released her, and she sat on the rim of the tub.

Jamal sat down next to her. "It's for you. This was your first basketball injury, so I thought that the treatment should be done up right."

"Aw, Jamal, that's so sweet," she gushed, then thought for a moment. "You're not going to try and get in here with me, are you?"

"No, although I'm sure that's really what you want me to do on some subconscious level." She rolled her eyes at him. "Let me see that foot of yours." She extended her injured leg. He put her foot into his lap and gently massaged it, lubricating it with the warm, soapy bath water. Catt closed her eyes and relaxed.

"Does that feel good?"

"Uh-huh," she moaned.

"There's still a little bit of swelling, but it should be gone by tomorrow." He gave her foot a few more deep caresses and set it back down. "Now, you go on and enjoy your bath. I'll see myself out."

"You're leaving?" she asked a little disappointed.

"Yes, you need to rest, and I need to think of what sport I'm going to whoop you at next."

"I guess you do. Anyway, thanks for everything, even for dragging me out of the bed tonight."

"Anytime." He brushed her hair back with his hand. "But you still suck at basketball," he chided. They both chuckled.

"You know a part of me really wants you to stay," she said softly.

"And a big part of me would rather stay here with you than go back to my own room."

"But we know that we can't do that," she reminded. "You better go."

"I can stay a little longer. What difference will another hour make?"

He tried to touch her, but she pulled away. "You know me and my Christian values."

He nodded and stood up. "Yeah, I know. I wish . . ." he began and his voice trailed off.

"Yeah, me too," she lamented. He didn't have to finish the sentence; she already knew what he was feeling. The mixture of anxiety, wonder, lust, and longing had made its way into her system as well.

"I'll call you in the morning to check on that foot."
He turned to leave. She abruptly called his name, and
he turned back around, hoping that she would ask him
to stay.

"What's up?" he asked anxiously.

She bit her lower lip and seemed to be struggling
with what she was going to say next. "I'm . . . I'm really
glad we're friends, Jamal. At least, I hope we are now."

"Is that all you called me back in to say?"

"No, but it's the right thing to say, so please leave
before I stop caring about doing the right thing."

"I'll leave but not because I want to. It's because I
want you to know that I value our friendship, and I respect your decision to stay platonic. So . . ." he leaned
down and kissed her on the forehead, "I'll talk to you
tomorrow."

He left with both of them wondering if they were in
deeper than either of them was ready to admit.

Chapter 22

"How's the foot?" asked Jamal the next morning, noticing that Catt was walking with a slight limp as they made their way down the elevator to check out.

"It's stings a little, but I'm okay."

"No doubt it hurts too badly for you to drive," he added sarcastically.

She thrust her luggage at him. "Or for me to carry my own suitcases."

The elevator released them.

"Just go to the truck," Jamal huffed, gripping both her luggage and his. "And you're driving all day tomorrow, no excuses!"

After loading the car, the two were en route to Milwaukee.

"Heaven . . . I wanna go . . . heaven," sang Catt along with Mary Mary as the up-tempo track poured in from Jamal's speakers.

Jamal raised his eyebrows. "Sure, everybody wants to go to heaven, but you know what they say."

She stopped singing. "What's that?"

"Everybody talkin' about heaven ain't goin' there," he quipped.

"Well, I'm going, I know that," boasted Catt.

"How can you know that, Catt? How can anybody know that?"

"I know because I've confessed I'm a sinner, and I believe that Jesus died on the cross to save me."

Jamal shrugged. "Okay, so do I. What does that have to do with it?"

She squinted her eyes in disbelief. "Are you serious?"

"Yes. I mean, don't you have to practically be some kind of saint to be guaranteed entry into heaven? You know, the kind who feeds the poor and helps old ladies across the street and goes to church at least three times a week?"

Catt was confounded. "Where are you getting your information from?"

"You hear things. Plus, it just makes sense. If you spend your life doing good things and depriving yourself of any real fun, you deserve to go to heaven."

"Based on your assessment, not many people would qualify."

Jamal looked over at her. "You would."

"I've made my fair share of mistakes too, Jamal."

"Like what—playing Shulammite woman for Stanley?"

"I can only wish that was my biggest mistake. At any rate, none of that has anything to do with getting into heaven. Salvation is open to anyone who'll accept it."

Jamal shook his head. "I don't think my soul is clean enough for all that. I've done too much dirt."

"There's no such thing as having done too much to be saved."

"Still . . . I don't know if I'm ready to start holy rollin' like you. I go to church once in every blue moon, and I enjoy a good sermon but, truth be told, I can't say I'm ready to stop sinning. I enjoy cussing and sex too much."

"If God was waiting on everyone to be perfect, nobody would receive salvation."

"You keep talking about salvation. What exactly am I being saved from—myself?"

"In a way, but specifically, from spending eternity in hell."

Jamal grunted. "The heat and I don't really get along that well, so what do I have to do to take a different route?"

Catt turned to him. "Answer this for me, Jamal, do you believe in God?"

"Of course, I do."

"Do you believe that Jesus is His Son and that He died on a cross for your sins?"

"Yes."

"Do you want the Lord to come into your heart and forgive your sins?"

"Yeah, but—"

She cut him off. "There are no *buts*. Do you want that, yes or no?"

"All right then, yes," he conceded.

"Congratulations! You've taken the first step toward salvation."

Jamal lifted his eyes toward heaven. "So just like that, I'm on the list to get in?"

Catt nodded. "Pretty much."

"So despite all the women I've been with, all the lies I've told, and all the dirt I've done, all I have to do is believe and I'm going to heaven?" He shook his head, not believing what he was hearing. "That's too easy."

"But it's true. Salvation is a gift from the Lord. It wouldn't be a gift if you had to jump through a thousand hoops to get it."

"It just doesn't seem possible. What about all those people who do unspeakable things—rape babies and kill people and all that? If they repent and confess their sins, they get to go to heaven too?"

"Salvation is for anyone who wants to receive it, but I have to believe that if Jesus is truly in your heart,

you won't do those things. We have a commandment
to walk in love, and once you're saved, you become a
new creature in Christ. Anyone who is outright evil like
that clearly isn't walking in love and hasn't received the
Spirit of the Lord."

"What if they do all that before they get saved? Once
they accept Christ into their lives, is all forgiven?"

"Yes."

He still couldn't wrap his mind around it. "It just
seems too easy."

"Don't drive yourself crazy worrying about the how
and why. Just believe."

Jamal surrendered. "Okay . . . I believe."

Catt exhaled. As they approached the off-ramp, she
said, "Pull over."

"What? Why?"

"It'll only take a minute, Jamal. I can promise you
that it'll be the best decision you've ever made."

"This better not take longer than five minutes." Jamal exited off the interstate and pulled into a long-
abandoned service station and put the SUV in park.
"Now what?"

Catt reached into her bag and pulled out her Bible.

"Do you carry that thing around with you everywhere
you go?"

"You'll be glad I did in a few minutes." She opened
the Bible to Romans 10:9–10. "Have you ever heard of
the Plan of Salvation?"

"I've heard of it. I'm not too sure what it is, though."

"Well, that's what I want to share with you today."
She laid the Bible between them so Jamal could look
on as she read. "If you declare with your mouth, 'Jesus
is Lord,' and believe in your heart that God raised him
from the dead, you will be saved. For it is with your
heart that you believe and are justified, and it is with
your mouth that you profess your faith and are saved."

"So that's it?" he asked.

"It depends. Do you believe what I just read to you?"

"Yes."

"Then repeat this prayer after me." She reached for his hands and closed her eyes. "Father God, I acknowledge that I'm a sinner in need of a Savior, and I believe God raised Jesus from the dead for my sins."

Jamal cleared his throat and repeated everything Catt said. She noticed that his hands were trembling as he spoke.

She went on. "I confess Jesus as my Lord, and I surrender control of my life to God. I receive Jesus as my Savior."

Jamal echoed the prayer and opened one eye. "Is that it?"

"Yes, welcome to the family! You're officially my brother in Christ."

He looked more anxious than relieved. "Okay, so what am I supposed to do now?"

"I think you should get baptized."

He wrinkled his nose. "Why? I don't want to sing in the choir."

"What?"

"I used to go to church with my grandmother when I was a kid. At her church, the only way you could say an Easter speech or sing in the children's choir is if you got baptized."

Catt burst out laughing. "No, silly. Getting baptized represents you becoming a new creature in Christ. Symbolically, it's the death and burial of your former self and the resurrection of who you are now in Christ."

"Oh. I'll have to get back to you on doing that one. What else do I need to do?"

"Find a local church to join, start reading your Bible, and try to live right."

Jamal sighed. "Basically, I've got to become you."

She pinched him. "Basically, you become who you are in Christ. Now, you have access to the Holy Spirit and all the power that comes along with that. Of course, you won't know what that is until you read the Bible and get up under somebody's teaching."

"So does this mean I have to stop having sex?" he asked nervously.

"It means you should. But if you slip, which you seem bound and determined to do, God's grace is sufficient to cover your sins."

He shook his head slowly, thoughtfully. "I suppose this is the part where I should thank you for saving my soul."

"You can thank me by saving someone else's. It's our responsibility as Christians to lead others to Christ."

"Can we get back on the road now or is there something else I have to do first?"

She giggled. "We can hit the road again. Hey, Jamal?"

"What?"

"I want you to know that I'm real proud of you for taking this step today. You didn't have to do it. In fact, I was half-expecting you to call me crazy or cuss me out for even suggesting it."

He shook his head and merged onto the highway. "Naw, I wouldn't do that, not to a friend."

She perked up. "So we're friends now?"

"Don't you think so?"

"We're definitely more than what we were those first few days in the lab."

"I was friendly. You, on the other hand . . ."

"I was what?"

He cut his eyes over to her. "What's another word for a female dog?"

She smacked her teeth. "I'm starting to think maybe all that salvation didn't take."

"That was many miles and moons ago, Catt." He playfully nudged her. "You're all right with your crazy self."

"You're all right with yours," she conceded.

Jamal became serious. "I think this trip has really changed both of us. If nothing else, I think it's changed the way we see each other."

"What's changed for you?" she asked.

"I finally realize the kind of person you truly are. You're a good woman, Catt, like that virtuous woman you were talking about."

She blushed. "That's sweet of you to say."

"In another lifetime . . ."

"What?"

He shook his head. "Things might've been different between us, that's all."

She nodded in silent agreement. She knew that by "things," he meant if *she* were different; specifically if she came wrapped in a smaller package.

For the first time, she actually knew what it felt like to be that quiet, fat fifteen-year-old who wanted nothing more than for the cute basketball player to ask her to the prom or to notice she existed.

Chapter 23

Catt looked at her chicken wrap and chucked it back into the paper bag it came in. "I'm sick of greasy fast food and eating out of the car. I need atmosphere and tablecloths and food that doesn't come in sacks!"

Jamal tried to balance the steering wheel and his fish sandwich as he rounded a bend in the road. "Don't worry—only 169 miles stand between us and the next stopping point."

Catt sulked. "I can't promise that my sanity and patience will hold out that long. I think I'm getting a little claustrophobic sitting in this car for hours at a time."

"Imagine how the driver feels!"

They whizzed by a clump of trees that made Catt stop and take notice. "Hey, there's a park!" she exclaimed. "Let's stop and eat there."

"You know how I feel about stopping, Catt."

"We're making good time, and I'm tired of being cooped up in this car," she whined. "Pull over."

"No," he stated sternly.

"Come on, Jamal. I need to stretch my legs, and we both need to be enjoying this beautiful day. There's a blanket in the back. We can make a picnic of it."

"A picnic?"

"Just pull over, all right?"

He grunted, then, seeing how eager she was, relented. "You think you're always supposed to get your way, don't you?"

"I usually do!" she added smugly.

Jamal swerved into a parking space. "Yeah, we'll see about me having *my* way later on."

They walked to a nearby picnic table directly across from a bubbling brook and a plot of grass where ducks roamed about the grounds freely.

Catt bent down to pluck an amaryllis. "Isn't it pretty out here? It's so peaceful and quiet."

"If you've see one park, you've seen 'em all." Jamal was still brooding about making the detour and getting behind schedule.

"Are you going to be like this all afternoon?" she asked him.

"I plan on it."

"Suit yourself. I plan to enjoy this beautiful day that the Lord has made." Catt walked ahead of him and spread the blanket out over the grass. She eyed Jamal, who sat on a nearby bench, transfixed on something.

"What are you thinking about over there?" she ventured.

He sucked his teeth. "Oh, you care now?"

"Not really, just curious."

"I'm trying to remember the last time I was on a picnic."

She thought back and sat down on the blanket. "I think the last time I went on one was when I got engaged. He proposed at sunset on a day just like today."

Jamal edged over to her. "What happened? With the engagement, I mean."

Catt bit her lip. "He cheated on me. I walked in on him and some slut a few weeks before our wedding. I don't think I've ever been as devastated and humiliated as I was at that moment."

Jamal joined her on the blanket. "That's deep. I can't imagine what that must've been like for you. I have to admit, I'm usually the guy who gets caught cheating or the one getting caught with someone else's girl."

"You should try being on the other side sometime. I guarantee you won't be as quick to sleep in someone else's bed."

"Is that why you're so hard on men now?" he inferred.

"I'm not hard on men, I'm hard on *you*. There's a difference."

"Well, is that why you're so guarded and closed off?" She didn't answer him. "Look, just don't take what he did personally. Men are stupid, present company included. We could have the best woman in the world, but the male sexual appetite is never satisfied. If a woman offers the goods, we have to accept. It's instinctual, I guess."

"The eyes of man are never satisfied," quoted Catt with a bitter laugh. "You say it's 'instinctual,' but *selfish* is what it is! Selfish and a cop-out."

"Hey, don't act like women don't get their creep on too, Catt."

"I know. It's selfish no matter who does it. I'm just thankful for the one or two good guys we do have out there who still believe in fidelity, like my father. My dad never stepped out on my mom."

Jamal raised an eyebrow. "You sure about that?" Catt narrowed her eyes at him. "Your dad may be a preacher, but he ain't perfect."

"He's a good man, Jamal. Don't put him in the same category as cheaters like you. It's insulting."

"And don't act like he's above screwing up on occasion."

"Whatever!" she muttered and crossed her arms in front of her.

Jamal tossed a pebble into the water. "Yeah, whatever . . ."

They were silent for a few minutes. Once the sting of his accusation wore off, Catt returned to her original question. "So you never did say when your last picnic was."

He shook his head. "I don't want to talk about it."

"You coaxed me into spilling all my secrets, but you won't spill yours? That's not fair!"

"Life isn't fair, sweetheart."

Catt fumed. "That's the last time I tell you anything personal."

"Fine by me. All I need to know about you is how well you can mix and sell a product."

She frowned. "You know, you have the uncanny ability to ruin a perfectly wonderful day."

"So I've been told," he replied, unfazed.

Two curious ducks approached them as they munched on their respective lunches. Catt broke off a piece from one of her wraps and gave it to them. She passed her lunch sack to Jamal. "Here, feed the ducks. Maybe it'll take you out of this funky mood you're in."

Two more ducks joined in as Jamal tossed a few morsels their way. "Who would have thought that I'd be spending my day in the country, feeding some ducks?" Jamal thought aloud. Catt giggled. He looked at her seated next to him on the blanket. "But I must say you *do* look happy. I never had you pegged as a country girl, though."

"Are you kidding? I love the outdoors, the sun, the smell, just feeling free without a care in the world." Catt seemed completely relaxed and at peace. "Did you spend a lot of time outside growing up?"

He shook his head. "Not really, not as much as I wanted to anyway, but we did have some family who lived near Lake Sinclair. We'd go out there a couple of times a year, whenever my dad could take off. Those

were the best times growing up," he remembered, tossing more bread crumbs to the ducks.

Just then Catt screamed as one of the ducks aggressively nipped her hand with his beak. She kicked at it,
but the other ducks immediately began to follow its
lead and surrounded them. She shrieked again and
jumped on top of the nearby tables as the ducks drew
closer. They began to assail Jamal too.

"What the . . ." he said, trying to shoo them away.
One duck squawked loudly and flew onto the table with
Catt. She screamed, dropped her wrap, and darted
across the park.

Laughing hysterically, Jamal took off after her. She
found safety at a nearby bench and settled breathlessly
onto it. He arrived a few seconds later still laughing,
holding what was left of their lunch and the blanket. "I
thought you liked nature, the sun, the air, the peace and
quiet," said Jamal, mocking her. "I wish you could have
seen your tail sprint across that path! I didn't know you
could run that fast."

She rolled her eyes at him. "You could have tried to
help me, you know," she snapped.

"Aw, girl, come here." He pulled her to him. She
leaned back against his chest as the two reclined hori-
zontally on the bench. "You know that I wasn't going to
let anything happen to you. I would have taken out all
those ducks: Daffy, Donald, Howard—all of 'em!"

A smile escaped from Catt in spite of herself. "All
right, you're forgiven." She sighed and stroked Jamal's
arms, which were folded around her. "This is nice. I
wish it could be like this all of the time."

"What's *it*—us?"

"Us . . . life . . . everything."

"So, you think that there really could be an *'us'*? If
our circumstances were different?" he asked.

"I don't know. I mean, we seem great together now, but being together day in and day out is something altogether different."

"Yeah, you're right," he agreed. "Marriage, living together—all of that changes everything."

"Besides," began Catt, "you're too doggone controlling, and you know that I couldn't have you trying to tell me what to do!"

"And you're too darn stubborn and sassy!" he shot back. He sighed and softened his tone. "Of course, I'd probably be willing to give up some of that control if I were with the right person," confessed Jamal. "You know, that virtuous woman you were talking about."

"And I would probably be more cooperative and submissive if I were with the right man."

They sat on the bench holding each other with hands intertwined, looking out onto the still lake. Words were not necessary and probably would have ruined the moment. These thoughts were to remain hidden in the heart, never verbalized. Talking about it would make the temptation to act on it too powerful.

Not wanting to get too comfortable in Jamal's arms, Catt rose and plunked their blanket down on the ground and rolled it out again.

"Why'd you get up?" he asked.

Catt shook her head. "It was getting a little too comfy for comfort."

"Guess I'm too much of a heathen for you to sit with me for five minutes," he joked.

"No, it's not that . . ."

"Catt, I'm starting to think the only man you can stand being around for any extended period of time is Jesus!"

"While there are some things I refuse to compromise on, I'm learning to be more flexible these days."

He agreed. "I have to admit it, you have chilled out some. If I could just get you to put the Bible down for two minutes, we'd be all right."

"I'm willing to do that if you tell me something else that I want to know," baited Catt. She propped her head up on her hands and stretched out on the blanket.

"What's that?" asked Jamal, joining her.

"I want to know about the nightmares."

"What, are you jealous because I'm not dreaming about you?"

She jokingly flung a stray twig at him. "No, I'm not *jealous*. I'm sure that more than one man is going home dreaming about Catt Cason tonight, but I'm more interested in your dreams."

Jamal leaned back and pinned his hands behind his head. "It's no big deal. I hardly even have them anymore."

"But you had one the other day. It seemed really intense. What were you dreaming about?"

Jamal sighed and murmured, "My mother."

"Your mother? I thought she was dead."

"She is. She died about three years ago, but I still think about her."

"You miss her," concluded Catt.

Jamal sat up. "No, I said I *think* about her," he repeated and got up to grab a soda.

"Umm, sounds like a story there," replied Catt.

"There's no story, not today anyway."

Catt was in no mood to argue with him. Instead, she closed her eyes and let the weariness of the day expel itself from her body with each breath.

"So, I came way down here to watch you sleep?" he asked as she dozed off.

Catt yawned. "I'm just resting my eyes for a few minutes. You stay on the lookout for any avenging ducks."

Jamal lay down beside her. "I think I could use a power nap myself."

They both dozed off, but were awakened by Jamal yelling "No!" and being startled out his sleep.

Catt sat up, alarmed. "You had another nightmare, didn't you?" Jamal exhaled heavily and disregarded her question. "I know that you had another one. You cried out in your sleep."

"I don't want to talk about that," he stubbornly replied.

"Why do you always shut down whenever I bring it up? You're going to have to talk about it sometime."

"I'm dealing with it in my own way."

"Yeah, with your women and your little accolades from work. But guess what, Jamal? It's not working. The demons keep coming back."

He knew that what she was saying was true, but he wasn't ready to delve into that turmoil, especially not now. "I'm fine. It was just a dream."

"Jamal, you're not fine!" argued Catt. "Why won't you let me help you?"

"There's nothing you can do because there's nothing going on. I just need to get out of here for a minute." He staggered to his feet. "I'm going to walk around a minute. I need to clear my head."

"You could talk to me," she suggested. "Jamal, tell me about these nightmares. What is causing you to jump up out of your sleep in a cold sweat?"

"Nothing," he mumbled. "I'm just stressed out about work. I need to be by myself for a while. I need to think."

"Then let me come with you," she pleaded.

"You can't. Catt, the place I'm in right now is so dark that I don't think you could handle going there with me," replied Jamal, defeated.

Catt touched his face. "I can try. I just want to understand you . . . if you'll let me."

He dropped his head. "Don't waste your time."

Jamal darted across the field, still hearing the yelling, the pleading, and the gunshot in his head. No matter what he did, stifling the images that haunted him
wasn't an option. They visited him every day without
fail. There were times when it was so overpowering
that Jamal would break down crying, covering his ears
and closing his eyes in a futile attempt to block it out
of his mind. Most of the time, he would try to distract
himself and repress the memories. Here lately, however, it seemed that he couldn't escape fast enough.

Catt's last words were still echoing in his head: *I just
want to understand you*, she'd said. But how could he
make her understand what he couldn't put into words
himself?

This was one part of himself that Jamal could never
understand. Why couldn't he just fall in love, be happy,
and enjoy life like everyone else? After his father's
death twenty-two years prior, it seemed as if he could
no longer relate to people in the same way, especially
women. Despite even Tonya's unwavering love and
loyalty, something in him would not let him give himself completely to her—or any woman.

He longed to be happy and at peace. He couldn't understand why this was seemingly more difficult for him
than for other people, but he did know that the reason was intractably tied to his mother, the yelling, the
pleading, and the gunshot.

Chapter 24

Jamal knocked on Catt's hotel room door prepared to dish out an apology. He barely spoke to her after returning from his walk and continuing the ride to Baltimore.

She opened the door and looked him up and down. "Yes?" she replied coldly.

"You can drop the attitude. I came to say I'm sorry."

Catt crossed her arms in front of her. "I don't hear you saying it."

"Can I come in first?"

Catt waited a few seconds before widening the door enough for him to pass through, then closed it again. "Now, you were saying . . ."

He faced her. "I'm sorry for the way I acted earlier. I know you were only trying to help. I was being a jerk, and I apologize. Hopefully, you can find it in your very loving and generous heart to forgive me."

"Are you trying to be funny?"

He sighed. "No, Catt, I'm being 100 percent sincere. I shouldn't have stormed off that way, leaving you vulnerable to another assault from the mob of angry, vindictive ducks."

She laughed in spite of herself. "All right, you're forgiven this time; just don't make it a habit." She sat down at her small table, which had pictures scattered across the top.

"Hey, what you got going on over here?" asked Jamal, picking up one of the pictures.

"I'm scrapbooking. I've been collecting pictures from all of the beautiful places we've seen. I wanted to go ahead and preserve them while the memories are still fresh."

He looked over at her photo album and noticed a picture of a little girl in afro-puffs holding up a fish. A man was crouching down behind her beaming proudly.

"Is that you?" asked Jamal, pointing to the picture.

"Yeah, that's me and my dad." She smiled and lifted the picture out of the album. "It was taken near my grandmother's house. I spent practically every summer there catching fish at the creek with my dad or running around with my cousins. I was about eight years old in that picture. It was my first fish." She handed the picture to Jamal.

"Sounds like you had the perfect childhood. I was lucky just to survive mine." He studied the picture. "They should have known you were going to be trouble even back then. What kind of little girl holds a dead animal like that with such bravado and pride," he teased.

"I was a sweet, adorable child," she bragged.

"Yeah, but I bet you went through that ugly phase as a teen."

"Who?" she scoffed and flipped through the pages until she came to one of a lanky teenager wearing a pastel-pink, bouffantlike gown with a red sash across the front and a tiara. She was holding a bundle of roses and standing on a football field.

"I'll have you to know that you are looking at Miss Sophomore for the Homecoming Court of Englewood High School. There isn't a drop of ugly on this queen!"

"I guess you were all right. You were a scrawny ol' thing back then." Jamal continued to look through the book.

"Don't hate just because your adolescence was plagued with acne and awkwardness."

"Please—I was *the man* in high school." Jamal stumbled across her senior prom picture. "I guess this was the boyfriend, huh?"

"Yes, his name was Jerrod Brown. He was our class president. We were madly in love and were supposed to get married and have a thousand babies," she reminisced. "Unfortunately, we broke up two weeks after graduation."

"He was a punk," grumbled Jamal.

"He was not!" she squawked.

"Look at him, that played-out fade, the lame tux. He couldn't handle you."

Jamal flipped to the next page. "Are they your parents?" He pointed to a young couple in wedding attire. The woman bore a striking resemblance to Catt.

"Yeah, it was their wedding day."

"You look like your mom. What does she do?"

"She rests in peace now. She died a few years back."

"I'm sorry to hear that. It's tough when you lose your parents. You become an orphan. You're no longer anybody's baby after that," he added. Jamal turned the page. A yellow piece of carbon paper was folded inside. He opened it and saw that it was a hospital receipt with *The Summit Women's Center* on the letterhead.

Catt instantly recognized the paper and snatched it from him. "I forgot that was in there." She balled up the paper and threw it in the trash. She seemed uncomfortable and nervous.

"It looked like it was from a doctor's office. Were you in the hospital?"

"It was outpatient surgery. I was only there a few hours."

"Why did you have to have surgery?"

"I just did, all right?" she said in a huff and closed the book before taking it from him.

"I wasn't finished looking at it."

"Yes, you were. It's time for you to go." She was flushed and trembling.

"Go?" he asked surprised.

"Yes, I don't feel good. I have cramps."

"You didn't five minutes ago."

"Well, I do now!" she insisted.

Jamal stuffed his hands in his pockets. "I guess you're having a Midol moment, huh?"

She flung her hand. "Whatever, Jamal. Can you leave now? I really don't feel well."

Sensing that she was anxious for him to leave, Jamal didn't press the matter. "All right, I'll see you in the morning. Get some rest," he said and left.

Catt walked to the trash can and smoothed out the receipt and looked at it again. She saw her name and that it was dated eleven years prior. Her eyes moved down to her height, weight, and other vitals, and stopped at the section classified as "procedure." To the right of it, the nurse had checked the box labeled "abortion."

She balled the paper back up and put it into the trash. She didn't want anybody to know, especially Jamal. Even if he accepted her having the abortion, he'd never understand about the child's conception. She'd thought that in leaving the university, she could leave that shame and those painful memories behind too but soon discovered that the past wasn't a place; it was a part of her that she could not escape no matter how far she ran.

Life had also taught her to guard her heart, especially with a man like Jamal, a rule that she was guilty of ignoring by getting dangerously close to him. She could feel herself starting to care for Jamal in ways that she shouldn't, but withholding her feelings wasn't as easy as it had been before she met him.

"Don't go there with him, Catt," she warned herself. "He can't do anything for you but hurt you. You can never let yourself get hurt like that by any man again. Plus, if he knew the truth, he wouldn't have anything to do with you anyway, not after what happened to Kennedy."

She recovered the receipt from the trash can again and decided to hold on to it as a reminder that she had to keep her guard up at all times or risk repeating the mistakes of the past.

Chapter 25

"You got everything?" asked Jamal, then strapped on his seat belt.

"Yep," replied Catt, buckling hers.

Jamal pulled out onto the highway. "All right. Looks like we can say 'adios' to Milwaukee."

"Not a moment too soon!" retorted Catt.

"You didn't like it here?"

"It's not the city. I'm just tired of riding. The irony is that I love to travel, but this is too much of a good thing."

"I'll make a deal with you. If you drive the rest of the way, I'll take you fishing. You can add that picture to your photo album."

"You just negotiated your way into driving us back to Charlotte!" Catt giggled. "I don't fish anymore. I haven't fished since I was a little girl."

"Fishing is one of the few pleasant memories I have from being a kid. My family was nothing like yours," he told her again.

Catt looked down at her hands as she spoke. "You know, um, what you said yesterday . . . it isn't exactly true."

"What did I say?"

"About me having a perfect childhood." She shook her head. "That's not true. I didn't—far from it to be honest with you."

"Obviously no childhood is perfect, but I'm sure yours came a heck of a lot closer to perfection than mine," declared Jamal.

"It's all relative, you know. My demons may not be your demons, but we fight them just the same."

He cocked his head to the side. "What demons could you have possibly had in the holy household of the Casons?"

"Just because my dad's a preacher doesn't mean we didn't have our share of problems. I believe the devil probably attacked us more because of it."

Jamal exhaled. "All right, I'll bite. So what happened to you that was so terrible?"

"We're a lot more alike than you think, Jamal. For starters, I had issues with my mother just like you did . . . I did something else too."

"You did what?"

Catt hesitated before answering. She bit her lips to keep them from trembling. Then she took a deep breath. "I killed my cousin."

Jamal swerved a little, not expecting to hear anything that traumatic. "*You what?*"

She nodded. "I told you, my life hasn't exactly been a fairy tale."

Jamal slowed the car down. "Okay, seriously, Catt, did you really *kill* your cousin?"

"In terms of legalities, no. Technically, I didn't kill him, but I do feel responsible for his death."

Jamal heaved a sigh of relief. "Why do you feel responsible?"

"It's like I said, my family has had its share of demons to fight. One of the biggest ones we've had to face is drug abuse."

"Drugs?"

"What I tell you goes no further than this car!"

"It won't. After all we've confided in each other, do you really think you have to tell me that?"

Catt braced herself to reveal a family secret that very few were privy to. "My mother was a drug addict, Jamal."

His jaw dropped. "What?"

"Yeah, it went on for a couple of years. I was young at the time and didn't really understand what was going on. My parents were living a different life then too. They weren't Pastor Jeremiah and First Lady Ola Cason during those days, just Jerry and Ola, two young, struggling parents who didn't know the Lord."

"Wow, I never would've guessed it. The way you talk about them, you would think they've always walked the straight and narrow."

"Not always, trust me. When they were younger, both of my parents were heavy drinkers and partygoers. I think my mom started dabbling in drugs shortly after I was born. She was going through postpartum depression. Rather than getting the proper help for it, she self-medicated with alcohol and drugs. At one point, it had gotten so bad that we had to move in with my grandmother. That's when I had the situation with my cousin."

"What happened?"

"My parents did a great job of hiding how bad things were from me. I mean, I knew that they were arguing about my mother spending all the money and hanging around strange people, but I was a kid. To me, drug addicts were *other* people, not my family members, *especially* not my mother. I knew she drank, and I knew she smoked. I just didn't realize it was crack."

Catt closed her eyes and thought back. "It happened during the time we were living with my grandmother. My grandmother kept my cousin Jimmy during the day while my aunt Debbie worked. He was a year older than me, but I was bigger. I was always kind of big and strong for my age.

"Anyway, one day, one of the little kids in the neighborhood asked if my mother smoked crack. The mere fact that he'd asked me that was enough to earn him a beat down. I guess he could sense that, because he wasted no time divulging his source of information. He said that Jimmy had been running his mouth, telling everyone who would listen that my mama was some junkie.

"I was furious! I couldn't believe that my own cousin was out spreading lies about my mother, and I was intent on making him pay for it. I tore out, combing the neighborhood looking for him. Eventually I spotted him throwing rocks into the ravine at the end of the street, an abandoned area in the neighborhood. A passing hurricane had just dumped several feet of rain into the city that week. As a result, the ravine had filled with water. The water was rushing down the creek to the mouth of a ditch.

"When I saw him, I made all kinds of threats to kill and make him regret the day he was born." Catt's eyes began to water, and her voice quivered. "I told him to take back what he'd said about my mother, to say it wasn't true. Then he told me he overheard my mother and grandmother arguing because Big Mama wouldn't give her any more money to buy dope. Then he said, 'My mama said Auntie Ola is a crackhead! I know it's true 'cause that's what everybody says.'"

Jamal placed his hand on her shoulder, giving her an out if she wanted to take it. "Catt, you don't have to—"

She shook her head. She wanted to go on. "I remember feeling this rage and anger that, 'til this day, I never felt before. I told him to shut up, but he kept taunting me and laughing at my mother. I pounced on Jimmy and wrestled him to the ground. I just wanted him to shut up!" Catt took a moment for herself. She closed her eyes and exhaled deeply.

"I remember wrapping my fingers around his throat as he thrashed about beneath me, trying to remove my hands and catch his breath, but I was relentless. I kept choking him, telling him to take it back. He managed to topple me and get up. Then he said something I won't ever forget."

"What did he say?"

"He said, 'You're crazy, and your mama's crazy too! That's why nobody is ever going to love you!' When he said that, something in me just snapped. I got up and attacked him again. I pushed him, and he fell to the ground. As he was lunging at me in retaliation, his foot slipped in the mud, and he fell down into the creek. He went underwater, engulfed by the rushing current.

"A few seconds later, he resurfaced and started yelling for help. He tried to fight against the pull of the water by grabbing onto the banks of the ravine, but it dissolved into his fingernails almost as soon as he touched it."

Catt stared out the window, pensive and somber, talking more to herself than to Jamal. "I remember looking down at him as he was drowning. Maybe I was too young or too mad to really understand what was going on. I told him to say he was sorry for what he said about me and about my mama. He tried to talk, but his mouth filled with water. Then a wave swept over Jimmy, causing him to lose whatever grip he had. He was soon flailing about in the center of the creek being dragged along by the raging current. He pleaded for help again, causing more water to flood into his mouth and choke him. Another wave washed over his head, and he was taken underwater again. This time, only an arm appeared above the water that seemed to be grasping for anything sturdy to hold on to. His head briefly resurfaced, and he seemed to be gasping for air but was immediately sucked back down. The strong current pushed Jimmy further down the ravine until he disappeared into the dark, gaping mouth of the large drainage tunnel."

Catt wiped her face, wet with tears, with the back of her hand. "I can still see myself watching, completely emotionless as Jimmy was being pulled to his death. It was a few minutes before something clicked inside of me to go get help. When it did, I ran and got my grandmother, but it was too late. Jimmy was already gone."

The car was stifled in silence. Jamal wasn't quite sure what to say, and Catt was doing all she could not to dissolve into a blubbering mess.

Jamal reached for her hand again. "Catt, it wasn't your fault. It was just a freak accident."

"Yeah, that's what everybody told me, but how can I not blame myself, Jamal? I shouldn't have attacked him. And I could've gotten help quicker."

"You were a kid!" argued Jamal. "You did what you thought was right."

"No, I didn't. I wanted something bad to happen to him. I wanted him dead for saying those things about my mother, and, at the time, I wasn't sorry that he died. I thought he deserved it."

"Have you talked to anyone else about this?"

"Of course. My parents had me in counseling for months afterward—we all were. In fact, it was Jimmy's death that made my mother see what her addiction was doing to our family. She sought help after that; we started going to church, and it was then that my dad heard the call on his life to preach."

"At least something positive came out of all that," he reasoned.

"Yes, I believe that having gone through and lived it gave my parents a powerful testimony and a stronger ministry. I just wish it hadn't happened that way. Even now, it's hard for me to face my aunt Debbie."

"Does she blame you?"

"She says she doesn't. Both she and my grandmother had been warning Jimmy about playing down at the creek for years, but it doesn't matter whether they blame me. *I* blame me!"

"But it wasn't your fault."

"I know that in my head. The heart is a different story."

"Catt, you're always talking about God and forgiveness. Don't you think at some point He wants you to forgive yourself?"

She ran her fingers through her hair. "You're right. My dad has been telling me the same thing for years. It's just . . ." She sighed. "I feel like I need to know that Jimmy forgives me, that he knows how sorry I am that I let that happen to him."

"I admit that I don't know as much about this heaven and religion stuff as you do, but I have a feeling that he does know and that he forgave you a long time ago."

A tear rolled down Catt's cheek. "If I could just talk to him one last time. There's so much I want to say to him."

Jamal looked over at her. "Why don't you trying talking to me?" he asked softly.

"I'm talking to you now."

"No, I mean, talk to me like I'm him. Pretend like I'm Jimmy."

She was puzzled. "What do you mean?"

Jamal pulled into the parking lot of a shopping center and took the keys out of the ignition. Catt looked around their surroundings. "Why are we here?"

"I trusted you when you led me to Christ. I want you to trust me now."

Catt pressed her lips together and looked him in the eye. "I do trust you."

"Good. Jimmy's gone, and you can't talk to him, but you can say everything you want to say to him to me. Get it off your chest."

She shook her head. "Jamal, that's sweet of you to offer, but you don't have to do this."

"Have you ever known me to do anything I didn't want to do? I know it's weird, but I think it'll help. Trust me . . . I've seen this done on TV."

"Wow, that really makes me feel better," she threw in sarcastically.

"Just try it. It can't hurt, right?"

"Okay . . ." She drew in a deep breath and squeezed his hands. "Umm, there's something I want to say to you, that I've wanted to say to you for a long time."

"Go on."

She looked at Jamal but projected Jimmy's face onto his. She could almost see Jimmy's heart-shaped face, dimpled cheeks, and fuzzy mane. "First of all, I want to say that I'm sorry. I never should have come after you the way I did. You weren't much older than me, and I know you weren't trying to be malicious. You were just repeating what everyone else had said.

"I was hurt because deep down, I knew you were telling the truth. No one wants to believe that their mother is a drug addict, so it's easier to kill the messenger. I think in my mind, I believed that if I could make you stop saying that, it wouldn't be true. I loved her so much, I didn't want to see her as anything other than perfect." Catt paused.

"Is there anything else you want to say?"

She nodded. "I'm sorry that I couldn't save you." Catt stopped to recant her apology. "No, I'm sorry that I didn't *do* anything to save you. Truth be told, at the moment, I wanted you dead. I didn't care that you had a mother and an older sister who loved you, that our grandmother adored you, or that you had a life and destiny to fulfill. I didn't care about all the people who would be hurt and affected if something happened to you. I wanted you to hurt the way I was hurting. I wanted you to suffer. I was so selfish. I know I was young, but that's no excuse.

"I want you to know how much I loved you, and there's not a day that goes by that I don't think about you and regret what happened that day. When I think about you down in that ditch in the dark, scared and cold, my heart breaks for you. I would do anything to take it back, but I can't. All I can do is hope that you've forgiven me.

"I want you to know that your death was not in vain," she proclaimed. "It was the catalyst for getting my mother clean and bringing us all closer to the Lord. My mother went on to be a powerful woman of God, and my father's church is growing every day. So many souls and lives have been saved as a result of his ministry. It in no way makes up for you losing your life, but you can take comfort in knowing that your life made a lasting impact on so many others. I just hope that, in spite of everything, you found it in your heart to forgive me."

"There's one thing you can still do," broke in Jamal. "You can forgive yourself."

"I'm trying to. It's hard. I can still see him going down that creek. I still hear him begging me to get help. I can still see his hand reaching for somebody or something to grab and grasping nothing but air."

"Do you remember what you told me about Kennedy? You said that she probably knows more about God now than she ever would have on earth. Believe it or not, that is a comfort to me. I know I don't have to feel bad or guilty about her not being here because I know she's in a better place. Why can't it be like that for Jimmy?"

"It's not the same. You did all you could to save your little girl. I practically did nothing to save my cousin."

"Don't you think I've gone over it in my head a thousand times? I've asked myself, 'What if I'd done something differently that day?' 'What if I'd taken another street and gotten her to the hospital faster?' 'What if I'd been more religious?' You can drive yourself crazy thinking about everything you did or didn't do right. I've just had to accept that some things are out of my control." He paused before going on. "That's why you have to have faith that God knows what He's doing."

Catt was stunned. "Did I hear you correctly, O ye of little faith?"

"I guess you're rubbing off on me," he admitted. "I look at you, and you're so strong in your faith and convictions. I can't help but think if you're this serious about it, there must be some truth to it."

Catt reached over and threw her arms around his neck. "Hearing you say that makes all the difference, Jamal."

He pulled away from her. "Now, I didn't say I'm ready to jump into the pulpit or nothing like that," he clarified.

"I know. I'm just glad to hear you say that you want to put more faith in God than you do yourself. That's what it's all about."

"What about you? Did you say everything that needed to be said to Jimmy?"

Catt nodded. "I think so. I don't feel like I'm carrying as much of the weight around anymore. Talking about it helped. I'd been keeping a lot of that bottled up since I was a little girl."

"I'm just glad I could be there for you." Jamal's smile lightened the mood. "So let's see . . . you told me about losing your virginity, I told you about losing my daughter. You saved my soul; I helped you make peace with your dead cousin. We've got less than a week left on this journey. Have all our skeletons exposed all there is to know about each other, or are there still a few surprises left to come to the surface?"

They looked warily at each other, but neither of them answered. They hit the road again in silence, wondering how many more secrets lay dormant, waiting to be revealed between Connecticut and North Carolina.

Chapter 26

"Do you know that this is the first Easter I can remember that I haven't been in church?" announced Catt over breakfast in the hotel's lobby Easter morning.

"Well, you've got a good excuse for not being there. It's not like you passed up church to spend the day in bed."

"There is no excuse!" contended Catt. "Resurrection Sunday is the most important day in the life of a Christian. It's the basis for our entire faith."

"Won't it still be the basis whether you're sitting on somebody's pew this morning?"

Catt tossed her half-eaten biscuit on the plate. "I still feel like I should be in church today. Correction—that *we* should be in church today."

Jamal shook his head. "Catt, we've got at least eight hours of driving ahead of us today. My plan is to check out of here by eleven, fill up the car, and be checking into our new hotel before 8:00 tonight. We've got a hectic schedule tomorrow, and I want to be well-rested for an early start."

"I don't think a couple of hours will make that much of a difference."

"That's because you're not the one doing the driving," he countered. "I hate driving at night. If we leave on time, we'll almost be there before nightfall."

"I think the Lord will bless us if we make the sacrifice and go to church."

"Have you noticed that you always throw in the Lord when you want to get your way?"

She exhaled. "Okay, I'll admit I have played the Christ card once or twice, but it's not like that this time." Jamal wasn't convinced. "I'll make a deal with you. If we go to church, I'll take the wheel once it gets dark."

"And how many times have you promised to help drive, then conveniently dozed off when it's your turn? No!"

"All right, so I've dropped the ball a few times when it comes to driving, but what I lack in driving assistance, I make up for with witty dialogue and thought-provoking conversation."

"That's debatable," he deadpanned.

"How about I promise to cook you the best meal you've ever had the second we get back to Charlotte?" she bargained.

"The meal I want the second we get back does not come on a plate."

She rolled her eyes. "Can you not be crass today of all days?"

"Sorry . . . old habits."

"Jamal, I'm not going to beg you. I'm perfectly capable of calling a cab to pick me up and take me to the nearest church."

"Be sure to let the cabbie take you on to St. Louis too, because I plan to be long gone by the time you get back."

She flung down her napkin. "Fine, I'll meet you in St. Louis."

Jamal rose from the table. "Do *you*, Catt. I'm going to go back to the room, pack, take a shower, and hit the road. I'm taking off at eleven with or without you."

She sulked but stood her ground. "I'm not afraid. The Lord will make a way."

"You better pray He does!"

***

Jamal returned to the lobby an hour and a half later to begin loading the truck. He spotted Catt talking to the front-desk clerk. "You packed?" he asked her.

"Actually, this very nice woman was just giving me the name of a church not too far from here," she replied, refusing to look at him. "A cab is on the way to get me."

Jamal let out a coarse chuckle. "Bullheaded 'til the end, I see. If you're doing this for theatrics, you can save it. Your time would be better spent bringing your bags down and putting them into the SUV. Checkout is in thirty minutes."

"I've arranged for a late checkout. I'm not leaving until after church, but thank you for the suggestion."

Jamal shook his head and started for the door. He dropped his suitcase and turned around. "Catt, this is ridiculous! Get your stuff and let's go!"

"I already told you, Jamal; I'm going to church today. You don't have to wait for me. I'll be just fine."

Jamal muttered something to himself and rubbed his temples. "I really will leave you. You do know that, don't you?"

"Yes."

"And no cab is going to drive you from here to St. Louis."

"I can book a flight if necessary."

"You don't even know how to get to the hotel we're registered at," he pointed out.

"That's what directions are for." She turned away from the desk. "Besides, Oni is supposed to be meeting us in St. Louis. If need be, I'll try to hitch a ride with her. You're going to be late. Better leave now if you want to make it there before dusk."

Jamal huffed, annoyed at how stubborn she was, and secured his luggage inside of the trunk. He returned to the front desk to check out and give back the room key. Catt was seated in a chair reading her Bible.

He strolled over to her. "Cab on the way?"

She didn't look up from reading. "It should be here any second now."

"Did you decide how you're getting to St. Louis?"

"I'll think of something. I'm very resourceful."

"It's not too late for you to change your mind. I'll even go up and get your bags if you want."

"No, thank you."

Jamal breathed out. "So you're really going to go through with this?"

"You're making it sound like I'm plotting to take over the world! I'm just going to church. It's Easter. I need to be there."

"You won't even know anyone there."

"I know the one I need to know." A horn honked outside. Catt peered through the glass doors and spied a taxi waiting out front. She tucked her Bible into her purse and stood up. "There's my ride. Guess I'll see you in St. Louis."

"I guess so." Jamal grabbed her and pulled her into a hug. "Get there safely."

"I will." She smoothed out her dress and walked out.

Jamal quietly counted to ten. He'd wagered in his mind that Catt was going to come back before he got to five. He had to hand it to her—she was nothing if not dramatic.

By the time five came and went, Jamal rushed to the door just in time to see the cab peeling off with Catt inside.

"She actually left!" he muttered in astonishment. Before the shock wore off, Jamal raced to the door to see in which direction the cab went, but he'd lost sight of it.

"Shoot!" he cried, then remembered the woman at the front desk. He dashed to the counter. "Excuse me," he said, vying for the woman's attention. "Can you tell me where she went?"

The clerk looked confused. "Who, sir?"

"The woman who was here a few minutes ago. She said you told her about a church . . ."

The clerk smiled in remembrance. "Yes, she was bound and determined to get to somebody's Easter service."

"Right . . . what's the name of the church?"

"I'm not sure which one she went to. I gave her the names of three."

Jamal cursed in frustration. "Did she seem more interested in one than the others?"

The clerk shook her head. "Not really. I just told her about the ones our guests frequent most often." Jamal pounded the desk lightly with his fist. "Have you tried calling her, sir?"

Jamal wondered why he hadn't thought of that. He whipped out his phone and dialed Catt's number. It went straight to voice mail.

"I should just leave her here," he muttered to himself, but he knew he couldn't. He wouldn't make it past the state line before guilt would lead him back to her. "Can you give me directions to the three churches?" he asked.

"Sure." The clerk drew out a map for him to follow. "The closest is Zion's Hope. I'd try that one first."

Jamal thanked her profusely and tore through the front doors.

"God, let me find her," he prayed quickly and uncertainly. He wasn't sure if God had taken to listening to him yet.

He strapped on the seat belt and pointed his car in the direction of Zion's Hope.

Twenty minutes later, Jamal discovered that the Lord does, in fact, answer prayers. He found Catt on the last wooden pew of the antiquated chapel. The church was little more than four walls, twenty rows of seating, and a small pulpit, but the congregation packed into the church appeared high in the Spirit. Even Jamal couldn't deny feeling the Lord's presence there.

He brushed past a couple to squeeze in next to Catt. She was so engrossed in the choir's jubilant singing that it took her a minute to notice he was there.

"What are you doing here?" she asked him in a loud whisper.

"Why do you think I'm here?"

"I don't know. You seemed quite adamant about getting to St. Louis on time."

He narrowed his eyes at her. "You knew all along that I wasn't going to leave you here, didn't you? We're in a church, you can be honest now."

She smiled a little. "I'll only say that I said a little prayer and asked God to soften your heart on the matter."

"Uh-huh," he grunted.

"But I am glad you're here," she gushed.

The more he listened to the choir minister to the congregation through song and felt the anointing of the pastor's words during his sermon, the more Jamal felt something move in his spirit. The pastor spoke of the glorious gift of salvation that Christians had received from the Lord and how it demonstrated God's deep love for His children. He reminded them that the blood of Jesus was strong enough to cover any sin.

Jamal became overwhelmed when he thought about the power in the name of Jesus and the tremendous sacrifice He made to save a sinner like him. It was truly a sensation he'd never had before. It was as if he were one with the presence of the Lord. The feeling of peace and love that enveloped him defied description. He concluded that this must be what Catt meant when she talked about having joy that could only come from the Lord.

At the end of the service, the pastor reminded the congregation that they were having an old-fashioned baptism in the lake behind the church and encouraged everyone to come out and support the candidates for baptism.

"Are you ready to go?" asked Catt once the benediction had been given.

"I don't know. I kinda want to stay for the baptism."

Catt was floored. "Really?"

"Yeah. Hey, you think you have to be a member of this church to get baptized?"

"Are you thinking about doing it?"

"I'm not sure yet. I mean, I remember what you said about it being symbolic of Jesus dying for us and dying to your old self. It just feels like something I ought to do."

"You can always get baptized when we get back," optioned Catt.

Jamal pondered it some more and shook his head. "I don't think I should wait."

Catt beamed. "If you're serious, I'll ask an usher or a hospitality member or somebody about getting you dressed and ready for baptism!"

She flitted about with a sense of urgency and excitement that Jamal had never seen before. He figured it must have been infectious because the church officials agreed to allow Jamal to be baptized despite his not being a member of the church once Catt explain their situation.

After being led to a small changing room and draped in white with the other candidates, Jamal hiked down to the creek to be baptized. As they approached the congregation, he could hear them singing, welcoming them.

"Let's go down, let's go down by the river," they sang. "Let's go down, let's go down by the river!"

Catt was among them, clapping and singing as loudly as anyone else. She kept a close eye on Jamal. Seeing her quelled the nervousness in the pit of his stomach.

A woman ahead of him stepped into the water, assisted by one of the church deacons.

The pastor extended his hand to her and proclaimed, "In acknowledgment of my sister's faith, I baptize you in the name of the Father, the Son, and the Holy Spirit."

He covered the woman's mouth and nose, dipped her back into the water, and brought her up again. The deacons quickly came to her aid to assist her getting out of the water and to offer a towel for drying off.

Jamal was next. He was always the cool, levelheaded one in a situation; this time, he was trembling as he was escorted into the water.

"There's joy . . . by the river. Let's go down, let's go down by the river," repeated the congregation. "Let's go down, let's go down by the river."

Jamal stood before the congregation, knee-deep in water and draped in white, his hands slightly lifted toward heaven. Watching him, Catt felt so full of emotion, she thought her heart might burst.

"In acknowledgment of my brother's faith, I baptize you in the name of the Father, the Son, and the Holy Spirit."

With that, Jamal went down into the water and rose a new being in Christ.

Catt clapped and rushed to greet him as he stepped out of the water. She threw her arms around him.

"I'm so proud of you," she whispered.

He blushed. "Thanks. I'm kind of proud of me too."

"Do you feel any different?"

"I do. Not 'I-want-to-go-out-and-save-the-world' different, but different." His eyes fell downcast. "You know, I never would've done that if it hadn't been for you."

"Don't give me all the credit. It was you who made the decision to accept Christ into your life. You also chose to get baptized. I just encouraged you."

"This trip has already changed my life forever. You do get the credit for that."

"I don't think either one of us is returning home as the same people that left from Charlotte."

Chapter 27

"Daddy, the most amazing thing happened today!" Catt rambled that afternoon to her father on the phone.

"Of course! That's what Resurrection Sunday is all about," he replied.

"No, I'm not talking about that—I'm talking about Jamal. Out of the blue, he decided to get baptized today."

"What brought that on?" Jeremiah asked, surprised.

"Well, we went to this little country church for service this morning and—I don't know—I guess the Spirit must've moved in him because he just announced that he was going to participate in the baptism." Catt sighed. "When I saw him go down into that water, Daddy, I felt so full, so proud of him."

"Wow, that's good. I'm glad you were there to experience it. It's always a blessing to be able to witness a new member being added to the body of Christ."

"There's so much more to Jamal than I gave him credit for in the beginning. He's introspective, kind, funny, and brilliant, just so many things," she blabbed.

"It sounds like you've turned a corner in your relationship. It wasn't even a month ago that we were binding the demons inside of him!"

"I guess I just needed a chance to get to know him," conceded Catt.

Jeremiah cleared his throat, not wanting to linger on the subject of Jamal too long. "Eldon tells me that the two of you had a wonderful time in D.C. I'm glad that you were able to run into each other."

Catt's enthusiasm waned. "Yeah, it was nice. I wouldn't call it life-changing, but it was cool."

"Oh, no love connection, huh?"

She could almost hear his smile crumble. "Eldon is a very sweet young man. He's just not what I'm looking for right now."

"And I take it that this Jamal is," Jeremiah stated.

"I don't know . . . maybe," she admitted for the first time aloud.

"Whoa, I didn't know things had gotten that serious!"

"They haven't, but I think this trip has changed both of us. It's challenged us in ways that neither one of us could've predicted."

"Now, I don't want you to go and get your hopes up, baby girl," cautioned Jeremiah. "You said yourself that this dude is a player. Of course, I'm glad to see he's making some strides, especially where his spiritual life is concerned. But unless there's been a supernatural cleansing and intervention, I'd hold off on him. Don't you remember Jesus' parable about the farmer and his seeds? The seeds that fell on rocky soil grew quickly but scorched when the sun came out because they had no roots. That boy doesn't have any roots yet."

"I don't have any illusions about us, Daddy, but I know he feels something just like I do."

"I still think your time would be better spent trying to get to know the minister a little better. He's proven to be faithful, to love the Lord, and to want to try to build a life with you. You would do well to sit up and take notice."

Catt gave in to appease her father. "I'll think about it."

"You do that, baby girl." He noted the time. "Well, I guess I better let you get back to doing your thing. You remember what I said, though! I know you're grown and you're going to make your own decisions, but I don't think this guy is someone you want to get caught up with. Keep it professional."

"I always do," Catt assured him before telling Jeremiah she loved him and hanging up.

Eldon knocked on Jeremiah's door and barged into his office. "Pastor, you may want to come outside and intervene. I think Sister Owens and Sister Jackson might come to blows! Little Tykeith kicked Gerrilyn's Easter basket, and her mother is ready to send Tykeith and his mama to their Maker!"

Jeremiah was so deep in thought that Eldon's words flew right over his head.

Eldon grew concerned. "Sir, is everything okay?"

Jeremiah shook his head. "I just got off the phone with my daughter. She was going on and on about this lab partner of hers. It appears that my Catt is rather sweet on him."

Eldon's heart dropped to his feet. "Are you sure?"

"Yeah, I'm pretty sure, and I don't approve—not one bit!"

"What are we going to do about it?" asked Eldon in a slight panic. "We can't let Catt get entangled with a man like that. He'll break her heart. Believe me, Pastor Cason, I've seen him in action. He's a womanizer. Catt deserves so much better."

"I tried to tell her that, but she's an adult, and she's out there on that road alone with him. She's gonna do what she wants to do."

"That's it? You're just giving up?"

"Son, all I can do is pray that the truth be revealed and that Catt does the right thing. That's all either of us can do at this point." He pushed himself out of the chair. "Now, if you'll excuse me, I've got to stop Sister Owens and Sister Jackson from turning Easter Sunday into the St. Valentine's Day Massacre!" Jeremiah left Eldon in his office.

Eldon was seething. Catt was slipping away from him, that much was apparent. And with her went his chances of becoming lead servant of Faith Temple. He needed something that would solidify his place in her heart and his standing in the church, but what?

His mind wandered back to the night he and Catt had gone to dinner, and she'd gotten drunk and came on to him. He snickered to himself—*who knew ol' Goody Two-Shoes had it in her? Most of the congregation probably thinks she's still a virgin; I did. Who knew that she was getting her rocks off behind closed doors?*

That's when the answer came to him. The solution was so obvious that he was almost ashamed of himself for not thinking of it earlier. What better way to secure himself in the Cason family than to give Jeremiah and Catt the one thing they didn't have—a son or daughter for Catt and a grandchild for Jeremiah.

The scenario played out before him like a movie in his head. He'd invite Catt to dinner and suggest that they have a drink. After all, what was the sin in one harmless drink? Only he'd let one drink become two, possibly three. He didn't want her completely intoxicated, just relaxed and in an amorous mood.

Then he'd take her home because she'd be too drunk to drive and offer to help her into bed. Stroke her ego—among other things—and with a little luck and the right timing, she'd wake up carrying his seed.

Of course, they'd have to come before the church and acknowledge their sin, especially once Catt realized that she was pregnant. But he was skilled at making speeches of the emotional variety. Jeremiah would almost insist that they marry right away to avoid Catt's humiliation and their actions hindering anyone's Christian walk. Once the baby was born, all would be forgotten and forgiven, and Jamal Ford would be a mere wrinkle in history that no one took the time to notice or care about anymore.

Chapter 28

Catt's face was still aglow with joy once they reached St. Louis and checked into their respective rooms.

Jamal put down his suitcase to unlock his door. He got a peripheral glimpse of Catt, who was grinning from ear-to-ear. "What are you so giddy about?" he asked.

"It's just been such a wonderful day, the best Easter ever!"

"I'm glad you enjoyed it." He opened the door and turned on the light. "I guess I'll see you in the morning."

She called to him just before he shut the door. "Wait . . . you don't want to stay up and talk awhile?"

He yawned. "I really am beat, Catt. It was a long drive, and I got *no* help with the driving." Jamal shot her a side-eye glance.

"I think I'm too wired to sleep right now. So many wonderful things have happened today."

"You could've burned some of that energy off by driving."

She rolled her eyes. "Good night, Jamal."

Impulsively, he leaned over and kissed her on the cheek. "See you in the morning."

A few hours later, Jamal was back at Catt's doorstep, much to her chagrin. By this time, the excitement of the day had worn off, and she was ready for bed.

"Look, Jamal, if you came over to drag me out to shoot hoops—"

"I had another nightmare," he blurted out. "I was sort of hoping we could talk about it."

Upon hearing that, Catt immediately flipped into nurturing mode. "Sure, come in." She tightened the belt on her robe and closed the door behind him.

Jamal sat on the bed. She wiped the sleep out of her eyes and plopped down next to him. "Was it the same as all the others?"

Jamal nodded.

"Tell me about it."

Jamal heaved in and out. "Just give me a minute, all right?" He was gathering his thoughts, trying to mentally articulate what it was that he needed to say.

"Take your time."

"This is not easy to talk about. I haven't told anyone the whole story, not even Tonya." He looked down at his hands and away from Catt like a scolded child. He was still searching for the right words to tell his story and expel his grief.

"What's this about, Jamal?"

"Do you remember that day at the park?" She nodded. "I had a nightmare. When you asked me about it, I just brushed you off. I wasn't ready to talk about it then. The truth is that I couldn't."

"Why not? We've told each other just about everything over the past two weeks."

"I know, but I guess at the time I didn't know whether I could trust you."

Catt pulled the comforter around her for warmth. "What about now? Have you changed your mind?"

"I have to tell someone," he asserted. "This thing is eating me up inside. I think the only way to get rid of these demons is to talk about it. That's why I came over."

"Go on," urged Catt, lowering her voice to an almost whisper.

Jamal closed his eyes for a moment. "I hardly know where to begin." He stretched out on the bed. "I guess the best place to start is with my father."

"Okay, well, start there."

"I've already told you how close my dad and I were. He was my hero, and I wanted to be just like him. I loved him. I loved my mother too, but the bond that my dad and I had was really special." Catt nodded, reached out and gently seized his hand.

"I guess part of the reason that we were so close is because most of the time it was just the two of us. My mom was always chasing her dream to be a singer. That was something she'd fantasized about since she was a kid, but she got pregnant with me at seventeen and got married soon afterward. She couldn't move out to L.A. like she'd planned, so she settled for whatever work she could get singing here and there. Most nights, she was performing at this club or that one until one or two o'clock in the morning. Every once in a while, she'd land a role in some musical, which also kept her out late at night. Then in the morning, she went to work and slept when she wasn't working. I didn't get to see a whole lot of her because of her crazy schedule. Of course, now that I have my own dreams, I can understand that drive, that passion to do something that you love. But, then, I just thought she was being selfish, so I clung more to my dad. Since she wasn't there much for him either, I think my dad really appreciated having me around. I think he needed me as much as I needed him.

"Anyway, one day, my mom came home with this dude, Leroy Bennett. I'll never forget him. He smiled too hard and always smelled like smoke and too much cologne. He introduced himself as my mom's *manager*. He went on about his record label contacts and the record deals he could get for her and all the money she was going to make. My mom had stars in her eyes and swallowed up all of it. Me, I don't think I ever believed him, not even then. I always knew he was a hustler. He just looked like he was shady."

"What did your dad say about all of it?" asked Catt.

"I think that he was probably feeling like I was, but he loved my mom. He *loved* her. He would've done pretty much anything to see her happy. He knew a career in music was her dream, so he went along with it.

"Anyway, a few months go by, and my mom was spending less time at home and more and more time with Leroy. He had her performing at different li'l clubs out in the sticks. It was always in juke joints that nobody ever heard of. She even quit her full-time job so that she could be available for him. Then she started being gone for days and weeks at a time with this man. I remember asking my dad when was she going to come home, and he would always say, 'Oh, she'll be here real soon. You know that she misses us and can't wait to be home again.' To this day, I don't know if he was just trying to protect me or trying to convince himself."

Catt hugged her pillow. "What was your relationship with your mom like at this point?"

"A little strained, I guess, since I didn't get to spend that much time with her. But when we were together, it was okay. That is, until she tried to get me to start spending time with Leroy."

"What happened?"

"When she wasn't working, she'd tell my dad that she was taking me to the movies or somewhere and when we got there, ol' smilin'-behind Leroy would already be there waiting. The two of them would be all over each other right there in front of me! I know that I was young, around eleven or twelve, but I knew what was going on. I hated them both for it, especially my mama because I knew how much my dad loved her." Jamal tilted his head and looked at Catt with ire. "You know that clown Leroy even told me that I could call him 'Daddy' when my pops wasn't around. I swear that just made me hate that fool even more."

"What about your dad? Did he know what was going on?"

"He had to!" reasoned Jamal. "Some nights, I'd hear them in their bedroom arguing. My mom would be screaming, telling him that he's wasn't nothing and that he was holding her back. Once, I heard her say to him that she was never going to have anything as long as she was tied to him. Then she would talk about all the crap Leroy had bought her and the places he'd taken her and everything he'd done for her. My dad would just listen and tell her how much he loved us and how we could still be happy together. He was a good one, though, because I probably couldn't have put up with that. I *know* I couldn't!"

"Sometimes it takes realizing that you'd do anything for a person to make you see that it's gone too far," Catt theorized.

"I guess so. This went on for a few weeks. Then one day, my dad and I went fishing. He would take me to this stream deep in the woods. It was always so quiet and peaceful out there, and it always smelled like pine trees. I loved it," narrated Jamal dreamily. He snapped out of it and continued the story. "We were laughing and talking when we got home that day. My mother was in the living room with suitcases packed. My dad asked her what was going on and if she had a singing gig out of town. She told him no, that she was leaving him and was never coming back. She said that she was going to marry Leroy and that they were leaving for California and were taking me with them."

"Oh my God!" gasped Catt. "What did he say?"

"He begged her to stay or at least to let me stay with him. I mean he was crying, Catt, no shame. At one point, he even got on his knees. She just shook her head and told him that he was weak, and that this proved it. She said that she wasn't going to let me grow up being weak like that. She wanted me to be a real man like Leroy. She kept calling Dad weak and saying that he wasn't a man. She even told him that Leroy was a better man in bed and that I was already calling Leroy 'Daddy.' After she said that, it just seemed like all the fight went out of him. He just stood there; he couldn't even look at me."

Catt shook her head. "I don't care how much she thought she loved this other guy, she didn't have to break your dad like that. Hearing words like that come from the person you love is enough to send anyone over the edge."

"That's exactly what happened. Right after she packed everything in suitcases and plastic bags, Leroy pulled up to come pick us up. I was crying and pleading with her not to make me go. I told her I wanted to stay with my dad. I kept telling him to tell my mom that I could stay with him, but he didn't. He just stood there." Jamal's eyes fell downcast. "He didn't say anything."

As he recounted the story, Jamal's eyes began to swell with tears despite his efforts to fight them back. "Then my dad walked over to the buffet table, opened the drawer where he kept his gun, pulled it out, and shot himself."

"Shot himself?" echoed a stunned Catt.

Jamal nodded. "One bullet to the head. My mom was completely hysterical, but I was numb. It felt like a dream or like it was happening to someone else. I mean, in a span of about thirty minutes, I went from a great time fishing with my dad, to hearing my mom announce that not only was she leaving, but that she was taking me with her, to having my tennis shoes covered with my father's blood as I watched him die right in front of me. How's a kid supposed to get over something like that?"

Catt dropped her head. "I don't know."

"One of them called the ambulance—my mom, I think, they came and pronounced him dead. Of course, ol' Leroy didn't waste any time. He had my mom take everything valuable from the house, and we were on a plane that same night."

"You didn't stay for the funeral?" she asked.

Jamal shook his head and wiped a tear. "I never even got to say good-bye. We were in California before the day was out."

"How did you end up back here?"

"Well, we were living out there, going from motel to motel, sneaking out to keep from paying. After awhile, Leroy's drug habit became apparent, and any money my mom did make from singing went into his arm or up his nose. He pawned all my dad's stuff, I think at one point he even had my mom turning tricks. Then he started beating her. I remember one time he beat her unconscious, and she had to go to the hospital. He never touched me, though, just ignored me. I couldn't muster enough sympathy to feel sorry for my mother," he recalled. "She took my dad away from me, and I hated her for that.

"Then one day, Leroy and all his stuff were gone. We didn't have any money or food and ended up having to sleep in women's shelters or with whoever my mom could convince to take us in for the night. Eventually, she got somebody to wire us some money for a bus ticket, and we came back to North Carolina."

"How long were you out there?"

"Almost a year. My dad had to die so that my mom could live with and get beat down by that fool for a year." Jamal began sobbing. Twenty-two years of repressed hurt, confusion, and anger all erupted at that moment.

Catt thought it best to let him cry. She offered her shoulder and held his head as he wept. More than anything, she wanted to hold him, to take him in her arms and erase whatever it was that made him hurt like that.

"Are you all right?" she asked when the sobs subsided and gave way to soft whimpers.

"Yeah," he said, lifting his head. "I'm sorry for just breaking down like that. I guess you probably think I'm crazy or something."

She shook her head. "I think you're wonderful and brave and that you have been holding this in for far too long."

He wiped his nose with the back of his hand. "Well, now you know it all, all of my deep dark secrets."

"I can't tell you what it means to me that you'd confide in me like this; that you'd trust me this much."

He looked into her eyes. "I do trust you. You're the first woman that I've trusted in a very long time."

"That means a lot to me, Jamal. I hope you know that."

"Yeah, I do."

Catt readjusted her position on the bed. "Is it okay if I ask you something? It's about your mother if you feel up to talking about her."

"Go ahead."

"What was your relationship like with your mom after everything happened? I mean, did you all just go back to normal, being mother and son? I know in our situation with my mother's drug abuse, it actually brought us closer together. Was it like that for you too?"

Jamal shook his head. "Not at all. For a long time, I didn't even speak to her. I rebelled a lot—started making bad grades, staying out, getting into trouble—just to hurt her. I had so much going on inside of me that I couldn't put into words, especially the rage I had toward my mother. Eventually, I started back talking to her again, but I knew we'd never be same. How could I ever get over that? At the time, I didn't have the option of counseling like you did. Perhaps if I'd gone, things would be a lot different, and I wouldn't still be dealing with this."

"So you haven't forgiven her?"

"I've dealt with it, you know what I mean? There's nothing anybody can do about it now. Being mad at her won't bring my dad back, and she's dead now too, so I just have to get over it."

"I think you need closure, like I needed with Jimmy."

"You want me to close my eyes and pretend you're her?"

"No, I don't think that'll work this time."

"Then what do you suggest?"

"I think there's a stop we need to make before we cross into Charlotte."

"Where to?"

She held his face in her hands. "To the cemetery. I think it's time you had a talk with your mother."

Chapter 29

"Whoo-hoo!" howled Jamal as he slammed the car door shut after climbing inside the SUV. "Next stop, North Carolina!"

"Thank God!" blurted Catt, who settled down in the passenger side.

Jamal feigned anger. "Oh, so you're getting tired of me, huh?"

"I'm getting tired of you, this car, these suitcases, and everything else you can think of that's associated with this trip!"

He laughed. "I feel you. I'm getting a little sick of looking at you myself." He cranked up the radio. "North Cack-a-lac-key, here we come!"

"You got to admit, it's been some trip."

"Yes, it has. One thing's for sure, there's not a thing we don't know about each other now."

Catt bit her lip and turned away.

Jamal took his eyes off the road for a second. "Why did you get quiet all of a sudden?"

"I'm sorry. I just zoned out for a minute. What were you saying?"

"I said it feels like we know everything about each other except our Social Security numbers."

"There are still a few hours left in the journey," Catt pointed out. "I may have those nine digits out of you before we cross state lines."

"With the way things have been going, you just might!"
Catt's mood turned pensive.

"Did you check out on me again?"

"No, I was just thinking."

"About what?"

"How much courage it must've taken for you to tell
me about Kennedy and your mother. Those kinds of
memories are not easy to relive, much less tell someone about it. I admire you for being willing to do that,
and I feel honored that you trust me like that."

"Well, Catt, you've kept it just as real with me. I know
it wasn't easy to tell me about your mother being on
drugs or to talk about your issues with your weight, but
you didn't hold anything back. That's what made me
feel like it was okay to confide in you."

"Really?"

"Yeah, I mean, you've been so open and honest with
me. I guess I didn't want there to be any secrets between us."

Uneasiness gnawed at Catt. She knew there was one
thing she hadn't confided in Jamal for her own reasons.
She'd worked so hard at being a paradigm of Christian-
ity that she was afraid of the real, ugly truth about her
past being revealed. But she knew that, as a Christian,
she needed to be transparent, and that meant telling
Jamal everything.

"Jamal, there is one thing I have been keeping from
you, but I don't want to anymore. I want to tell you
the truth, I want to tell you everything," began Catt.
"Maybe, then, my nightmares can stop too."

He was taken aback. "*Your* nightmares?"

"Yes, there are things in my life that I've been dealing with for years. You know Jimmy is one. That yellow
piece of a paper is another one."

"What yellow piece of paper?"

"Don't you remember that day in my hotel room when you were going through my scrapbook?"

"Yeah, what about it?"

"There was a hospital receipt in there that I didn't mean for you to see."

"I remember. You seemed sort of freaked out about it."

"With good reason," she said. "It's not something I like to think about, much less talk about."

Jamal shook his head. "I don't get it. You said you had outpatient surgery, so what's the big deal? It wasn't anything life threatening, was it?"

"No, but what happened was just as devastating." Catt reclined the seat back and unleashed her saga. "It was senior year of college, around October."

Jamal turned down the music. "What happened?"

"My roommate, Keila, and I were thick as thieves, always getting each other into or out of trouble. Sometime around September, Keila started dating this guy named Jarvis who she'd met at a party one night. A couple of weeks later, he invited her to come to a house party with him. She was a little reluctant because it was out of town. She begged me to tag along, but I was hesitant. I mean, she barely knew Jarvis and knew even less about the people that would be at this party. But I agreed to go with her, against my better judgment. If nothing else, I thought, we could go and keep each other safe."

Catt stopped as if she were deep in thought and had just recalled a painful memory. Jamal pressed her to continue the story.

"On the night of the party, Jarvis came to pick us up, and we drove around for about an hour looking for the house. Eventually, we found it. Then we went inside. It was very dark except for a black light and maybe one or two candles. Everybody was hugged up—kissing, doing whatever. It felt like we had just walked into some big orgy. It didn't take long for Keila and Jarvis to blend right on in. In fact, I lost track of them once we got inside.

"Anyway, I sat down on the sofa, and a guy came over to where I was. We started talking and drinking . . . *a lot of drinking*," she stressed. "After a while, I guess I just got caught up in everything that was going on, and we started kissing and things started to heat up. He told me that there was a basement in the house that we could go into for more privacy. I agreed to go, but by this time I was really drunk. I mean, I could barely walk, so I told him that I wanted to stay upstairs on the couch instead. He started insisting that we go, and he hoisted me up and carried me downstairs."

"Were you drugged or something?" Jamal asked concerned. "He could have put something in your drink."

"I don't know, I suppose it's possible since he was the one bringing me the drinks. Anyway, the next thing I know, we're on a bed. He was touching me and trying to take my clothes off. I don't know if I actually told him to stop, but I do know that I wanted him to. I felt confused and like I couldn't move or speak. I was just totally out of it. I remember him climbing on top of me, and I sort of blacked out after that. I'm not really sure what happened.

"When I woke up briefly, Keila was helping me get into the car, and the last thing I remember is waking up in my own bed the next day."

"And you have no idea who the guy was? Did you have a name or anything like that?"

"He told me his name, but I can't remember it. I just know that it was something 'dre, like Deondre or Keondre. Then again, he could have made it up."

"All right, tell me what happened next."

"That morning when I asked Keila about it, she said that she and Jarvis were looking for me so that we could leave, and that she found me alone and naked in the basement. She dressed me, and they had to help me to the car and into our apartment. She wasn't sure what happened while I was down there. I assume that some students from school were at the party because by Monday, the whole campus was buzzing about how I'd slept with a bunch of guys at the party."

"What?" he exclaimed.

Catt nodded. "You can imagine how I felt and what was going through my head. I didn't know what to think— had I been raped? Did I really let those guys do that to me? Was it true?" She lowered her head and seemed to be fighting back tears. "It was horrible."

"Maybe nothing happened, you know?" suggested Jamal to make her feel better. "Maybe the guy saw how out of it you were and left. Someone probably saw you go down there with him and just assumed that something happened. You know how people just make stuff up to have something to gossip about."

"No, something definitely happened," she assured him.

"How can you be sure if you don't remember?"

"I had proof. You see, a few weeks later, I went to the doctor to have an AIDS test just to put my mind at ease. My biggest concern was that I might have acquired some kind of disease from someone at the party; I hadn't really considered the possibility of anything else being wrong with me. The HIV results came back negative, but the other test didn't."

"What test was that?"

She took a deep breath. "My pregnancy test."

"Catt . . ." Jamal was at a loss for words. He slid his hand into hers and listened as she went on.

"I could have died right there when the doctor told me. I was alone, scared, and pregnant. Worse than that, I had no idea who the father was."

"So what happened to the baby?"

"At the time, I felt like I couldn't go through with the pregnancy. I couldn't fathom keeping the baby. I was still trying to deal with what happened that night. So I had an abortion and never told anyone except Keila, who took me to have the surgery." She looked up at him. "You probably think I'm a monster."

Jamal was befuddled. "Why would you say that?"

"You lost your baby. You had to watch your child, a piece of you, die right there in front of you. I let them kill my baby, and why? Because I wanted to finish school? Because I didn't want my parents to know what happened? It was selfish. My baby didn't deserve to die regardless of how he or she was conceived."

"Catt, you were violated! I don't condemn you for having an abortion. If I were in your situation, I probably would've done the same thing. Please don't feel like what you did somehow makes you a lesser person in my eyes." Jamal enclosed his hand over hers and kissed her palm. "You're so strong to have gone through what you have and not let it get the best of you. I've always admired and respected you but never as much as I do now. You don't have anything to feel ashamed about."

"Thank you for saying that, Jamal. Knowing that you understand why I did what I did helps me more than you know."

"Catt, I had no idea you'd gone through anything like this. Please forgive me if asking you to talk about it has dredged up a bunch of bad memories for you."

"It's nothing you said or did. I live with these memories every day. Like you, hardly a day goes by when I don't think about my child that I aborted. I guess that's why I've held on to that hospital receipt for so long. It's the only thing I have that proves the baby existed, even if it is the very thing that proves that I allowed my baby die."

"You did what you thought you had to at the time. I honestly don't know how you got through it all."

"It was tough for a long time," she admitted. "After all of that, I was in a completely depressed state. Most days, I didn't even get out of bed. I just ate and cried. That's when I ballooned to the size I am now. I know somebody had to be praying for me. God's grace and mercy are the only things that kept me from losing my mind."

"Didn't your folks or your friend notice that you were depressed?"

"Sure they did, but what could they do? I refused to talk about what was going on. All they could do was ask God for a breakthrough on my behalf and have faith that I'd come out of it."

"I'm surprised you felt like you couldn't talk to anyone about it, especially your parents. You and your dad seem so close."

"We are, but this was something I couldn't even talk to him about. I think I was afraid that they would've blamed me for what happened and condemned me for having the abortion."

"I hope that you don't blame yourself for what happened."

"How can I not blame myself, Jamal? I was the one who went to the party, I was the one who got drunk with some guy that I didn't even know; and I was the one who killed my baby."

"What happened to you was a crime, Catt. Even if you didn't tell the guy no, you were under the influence, which still makes it rape. If there were other men, they certainly didn't have your consent."

"For all I know, I might *have* consented. I may have even initiated it, I have no proof to suggest otherwise."

Jamal gripped the steering wheel with his left hand to free the right hand to envelop hers once more. "Catt, I know I wasn't there, but I know you. This wasn't your fault. You were victimized in the worst way imaginable, and nobody has paid for it except you. It's just not right." He thought back. "I remember that night I came by to play basketball with you, and I made a joke about seducing you in your sleep. You got upset and I couldn't figure out why. Now, I understand."

"I know you do, and I know that you didn't mean anything by it when you said it."

"I'm glad. I just wish you had told me sooner."

Her eyes watered. "There were many times that I came close, but I was scared," Catt confessed.

"Scared of what?"

"I was afraid of how you'd react, of how you'd look at me after you knew the truth."

"Catt, you are such an amazing person. How could I look at you and see anything other than that?" he asked, wiping a tear from her cheek.

"Then why can't I see it?"

"You've had the worst thing that can happen to a person happen to you. As a man, I'll probably never know what that's like, but I do know that if you let them get in here and change who you are, they will have won. Don't give them that victory, Catt."

"It's just been so hard. That night took so much from me, Jamal, some of which I don't think I've ever gotten back. That's probably why I stay so involved with my work and the church. It gives me an escape and allows me to be in the world without letting anyone get too close. I've spent so much time building this wall that I don't know what else to do or who to trust anymore."

"You can trust me. And when you don't know what to do, just lean on me and we'll figure it out together."

He reached across the seat and pulled her to him. She rested her head on his shoulder. "Okay."

"And I don't want you blaming yourself for what happened, you hear me? And don't ever think that you aren't worthy." He kissed her on the forehead. She closed her eyes and let herself be comforted.

Chapter 30

It was their last night, the last time they would be together like this. They decided to go dancing for a change and found an intimate jazz club at the end of a long Memphis street. After nibbling on scallops and crepes with a glass of wine for dinner, Jamal and Catt headed back to the hotel.

Jamal walked her to her door, both of them anticipating what would happen next. "Are you about to turn in for the night?"

She shook her head. "I'm not really that tired. What about you?"

"I'm not sleepy either." His eyes fell to the floor. "I was sort of wondering if you wanted to let me come in for a minute."

Catt's heart rate sped up. "Umm . . . okay. I suppose that'll be all right." She unlocked the door and let him in.

Jamal seemed almost as nervous as she was. He picked up the remote control. "You want to watch something on TV?"

"If you want to."

He tossed the remote aside. "Nah, I'm not really in that kind of mood right now."

"What kind of mood are you in?"

Jamal shrugged. "We can just talk if you want."

"Okay."

He sat down on the bed and invited her to join him. "Catt, I want you to know this has been the trip of a lifetime for me. I know it was supposed to be about meeting our sales goals and promoting Telegenic, but the only part I'll remember years from now is time I spent alone with you."

"It's been very special for me too, Jamal."

"I've never met anyone like you, Catt. You're smart, funny, and easy to talk to." She mentally noted that he left out sexy or beautiful.

"I'm glad we've had this time to see each other for who we really are. You know, initially, I thought you were a pompous, arrogant, misogynistic creep." She snickered. "I don't think you're misogynistic anymore."

Jamal pretended to be offended. "Oh, you got jokes, huh?" He seized her and teasingly tussled her down on the bed.

Catt shrieked with laughter. "I'm kidding, all right! You're cool!"

"That's better." He let her go. Jamal's playfulness turned serious. "Honestly, I can't believe you're still single."

She smiled up at him. "I'm still waiting for God to send me the man He wants me to have."

"Sometimes, you can't just wait for things to happen. Every once in a while, you've got to take the initiative." He curved his hand around her face. "Like now . . ."

Jamal drew Catt's face into his and pulled her into a lip-lock. His kiss permeated through her whole body. The look in his eyes and the deep thrusting of his kiss solved the mystery of what he had in mind. The remaining question was whether Catt would take the bait.

Catt was the first one to pull away. "What was that for?" she asked surprised.

"I just felt like kissing you. I've been feeling like that a lot lately." He drew her in for another kiss.

Catt broke away again. "This is so cliché."

"What is?" asked Jamal, still holding her.

"Us, slobbing each other down in my hotel room like a couple of horny teenagers."

"Would you prefer my room?"

She socked him in the arm. "Jamal, you know what I mean. To top it off, this just confirmed the theory that men and women can't be friends without sex being involved."

"So is sex going to be involved?" he asked hopefully.

She parted her lips to speak but didn't know what to say. Yes, biblically, she knew what to do: flee the devil; resist temptation; don't have sex outside of marriage. But there was a part of her that longed to be kissed and held and made to feel like a woman.

"Jamal, let's say, hypothetically, that if something were to happen between us tonight, what happens in the morning? Can we go back to normal after that?"

"I can, but can you?"

Catt pondered the question but didn't have an answer to give him. "You see, this is why I wanted to stay platonic," insisted Catt.

"You don't think this is platonic?"

"Far from it! This was not supposed to happen."

"What?"

"This . . . everything being all complicated like this. I just wanted to be your friend, Jamal."

"You don't think we're friends?"

"Of course we are. I just wasn't expecting to feel this way about you. You know my brain is telling me to run and get out while I still can."

"So I take it that your feelings for me run a lot deeper than just the brother/sister dynamic that we've tried to create over the past few weeks?" He waited for a reply from her. "It's okay, Catt. My feelings for you have taken me to places that I wasn't expecting either, but I don't think we should run from what's happening between us."

"I'm glad to know it's not just me." She smiled nervously at him, relieved to have finally come out and said what she was feeling, but was clueless as to what to do about it.

"So . . ." he traced the outline of her neck with his finger. "Are we gon' do this or what?" He brushed his lips across her lips. "I know it's crossed your mind at least once."

"It has," she admitted. "But I don't want to do anything we might regret later on."

"Catt, it's one night, our last night together. I feel like we've gotten closer over the last three weeks than some people do in a lifetime. Let's just have our night and see what happens."

She wrapped her hands around the back of his head. "I don't know . . ."

He stroked her hair. "You know, I meant what I said earlier. I think we should see this thing all the way through and find out where it takes us."

"What if we look at each other tomorrow and wish we never did it."

"Just live in the moment, Catt. That's what this whole trip has been all about." He braided his hand into hers. "Live in the moment."

She tilted her head to face him and placed a soft, tender kiss on his lips. She felt her biblical and moral standards slipping with every kiss that passed between them. But somewhere in the back of her mind, she knew that something bigger was at stake than her libido at that moment. As much as she wanted to be with Jamal in every way, she knew she couldn't.

He felt her pulling away. "What's wrong?"

She sighed and sat up. "I can't explain it. Being with you just feels right to me, but I know it's wrong."

The disappointment registered on his face. "Does this mean you're having second thoughts?"

"I don't want this to change things between us, but I know it will. And, as much as I want to be with you, I can't compromise my principles for anyone."

Jamal exhaled and gave himself a minute for the fires to burn out of his system. "Okay, I can respect that."

"Are you mad at me?" she asked warily.

"Let down is more like it," he revealed. "But I've been turned down before and much further along in the process! It's cool." He planted a kiss on her forehead. "You want me to leave?"

"No, unless that's the only reason you came over."

"I came because I wanted to spend my last night with you whether we're watching TV or watching each other naked."

She laughed. "I think we should try doing the former."

He grabbed the remote and cradled her in his arms. "You okay?"

She nodded. "Better than okay. In fact, I can't remember the last time I was this happy." She wrapped her arm around him. "What about you? How are you feeling right now?"

"I'm good, better than I've been in a long time."

"You ready for tomorrow?"

"What—when we get back to the real world?" he asked. "Yeah."

"Let's think about tomorrow, tomorrow. For now, let's live in the moment."

Chapter 31

At Catt's insistence, Jamal wound up at the very place he'd once vowed to never return to again following his mother's funeral and burial. Up until this point, he'd made good on his promise.

"Watch your step!" cautioned Jamal as they trekked their way through the neglected cemetery. It was overgrown with brush and thorns and was barely visible through the undergrowth. It looked like the kind of place where people buried relatives they had all intentions of forgetting once the funeral was over.

His father's decaying headstone was next to his mother's and in just as bad a condition. He used to visit his father's burial plot whenever he felt lonely or longed to be close to his father but stopped once his mother's body had been placed next to it.

Catt stooped over her headstone and swept aside the leaves and dirt that concealed her name. "Are you ready?" she asked Jamal.

Jamal nodded and kneeled down beside her. "This feels weird to me."

"Just talk to her. Tell her what you want her to know . . . good or bad."

Jamal started to say something and stopped several times before finally breaking his silence. "I know you're probably wondering what I'm doing here," he began, addressing his mother. "'Why now?' To tell you the truth, I don't really have an answer. It seems strange, you know—being here with you and Daddy, yet not being with you at the same time." He looked up at the cloudless sky, picturing them in heaven looking down on him.

"Have the two of you been watching over me all this time? Have you seen my little girl? I guess it's some comfort knowing she's up there with family." He gave himself a moment to let the pain of remembering Kennedy pass.

He addressed his mother again. "Most all my life I've hated you. I thought that you were the most selfish person that ever walked this earth. First for abandoning us to chase after your dreams, then for leaving Dad for Leroy, only to have him beat and misuse you in the end. Mostly, I hated you for taking my father away from me. You didn't pull the trigger, but you might as well have. You didn't love him, not like a wife should love her husband, and it destroyed him. And me—I was just a kid. I didn't deserve to get all caught up in your bull." He shook his head as he reflected on the mess that her actions had made in all of their lives.

"But I'm not a kid anymore. It's only now that I'm finally able to understand what life must have been like for you. The way you felt about music, the way it moved through you and became a part of you; that's the way I feel about what I do. I can't suppress that any more than you could suppress your voice. I even understand the way Leroy made you feel, how he made you come alive and look forward to waking up every day because that's how Kennedy made me feel. And I know why you had to leave Daddy. The marriage was choking you. You married him because you had me and you felt like it was the right thing to do. Maybe it was right for me but not for you. I know what it's like to go into a marriage with the best of intentions and it still not work out. Tonya was the kindest and most devoted person I've ever known. She was an excellent mother and tried to be a good wife to me. But you can't make yourself feel something that isn't there. Whatever magic we had died when Kennedy did." He broke off a weed and flicked it into the air.

"And it wasn't all your fault. Looking back at it, I have to acknowledge that Daddy had some serious issues of his own. Why else would he have been driven to take his own life or not let you go when he saw that you were so miserable? I don't hate you now, and I forgive you for any part you had in my father's death. I just wish that I hadn't wasted so much time being angry. I have peace with the situation now, and I forgive you." He placed his hand gingerly on the tombstone. "I forgive you."

"How do you feel?" asked Catt.

"Relieved, like this weight I've been carrying around since I was fourteen has finally been lifted."

"That's how it is when you cast all of your burdens over to the Lord. 'Cast all your cares on him because he cares for you.'"

"One day, I hope I can be as strong in my faith as you are in yours."

"You will be," promised Catt. "Once you realize that you can trust God and that He loves you so much that He'll never leave or forsake you, you won't have any problems trusting Him."

Jamal placed his hand in Catt's and led her out of the cemetery as they prepared to make their last stop. Either the return to Charlotte would signal the end or be the first step to their new beginning.

Chapter 32

The last ten minutes of the ride to Catt's house was spent in silence. So much had happened since they first backed out of her driveway, and neither of them quite knew what would happen once they returned to the normal lives and routines and, in Jamal's case, lovers.

Jamal rolled into her driveway just as rain began to pelt the roof. He put the SUV in park. "Well, I got you home in one piece."

She nodded. "Yes, you did."

An awkward silence took the place of dialogue. Jamal stared out of the windshield. "So now what?"

Catt looked down. "I don't know. It feels like we're in unchartered territory now. It's like we've said and done too much to go back, but no one knows how to move forward."

Jamal agreed and squinted his eyes, looking up at the sky. "I better start unloading the truck. It looks like it's about to pour down."

She seized his arm. "Jamal, wait."

"What's up?"

"I just wanted you to know that I think you're a good man. I know I haven't always felt that way, but I do now. I've watched you grow into a better person in every way over the course of this trip, and I feel blessed to have been able to witness it."

"I appreciate that." They watched the rain splatter and roll off of the windshield. "You know I never really thanked you," he reminded her.

"Thank me for what?"

"Everything. Whether or not I was willing to admit it, I was a mess before this trip. Yeah, I had the good job, the women, and the outward artifacts of success, but I was screwed up inside. You helped me change all that, and I'll always be grateful."

"That's what friends are for, right?" She wrung her hands together. "And what about the other night . . ."

He smiled sheepishly. "No need to explain, Catt. It was late, and we were tired. I think we were both out of our heads a little bit."

"What would you have done if I hadn't stopped you?"

"I probably would have stopped myself before things went too far."

"Why?"

"Because . . . we're friends, Catt. Like you, I don't want to screw that up."

She played with his fingers, weaving them in and out of hers. "What makes you so sure that it would have been a bad thing?"

He gazed down at her. "What's up with all the questions, Catt? Nothing happened—that's all that matters."

She shrugged. "I just . . . maybe it wouldn't have been a *complete* mistake, that's all."

"What are you saying?"

"I'm not sure."

"I think you are. Come on—what's on your mind?"

She took a deep breath. "I was just thinking that maybe sleeping with you wouldn't have been the worst thing in the world . . . maybe it would have been sort of nice."

Jamal felt warm all over. "You know, if I didn't know better—"

"What?" she butted in.

"Do you want me to come in?" He inched toward her for a kiss.

They sprang apart before Catt could answer, startled by a horn honking behind them. Catt turned around and saw her father's Lincoln parked behind them.

"That's my dad," she informed Jamal.

"Were you expecting him?"

"No."

"Are you going to send him packing?"

"No, Jamal! That's my dad. Get out. I want you to meet him." Catt stepped out of the car into the rain, and Jamal reluctantly followed. She covered her head with a newspaper lying on the seat and raced to her father.

"Daddy!" she cried and threw her arms around his neck. "I missed you so much!"

Jeremiah hugged her. "I missed you too, baby girl!"

Eldon emerged from the passenger side of the car. "We're glad to have you home safe and sound."

"It's good to be home." Catt pulled away from her father. "Eldon, hi. How nice of you to come by." Jamal stepped forward and stood at her side. "Daddy, this is Jamal Ford."

Jamal extended his hand to Jeremiah. "It's good to finally meet you. Your daughter speaks very highly of you. I can tell she loves you very much."

Jeremiah thanked him. "It's nice to finally put a name with the face. Catt tells me you two had quite the adventure out there."

"We did." Jamal and Catt exchanged wistful glances. "But all good things come to an end."

"We need to get out of this rain!" bellowed Catt. "Daddy, can you grab my bags while I unlock the door?"

"I'll do it," said both Jamal and Eldon in unison.

Jeremiah cleared his throat. "That's okay. I'll do it. Is the trunk unlocked?"

Jamal popped the trunk with the keyless entry.

"Minister, why don't you go in with Catt to make sure everything is just as she left it?" suggested Jeremiah, heading to Jamal's SUV.

Catt turned to Jamal. "Are you coming in too?"

Jamal considered it, but their moment had passed. "Nah, you go on in and enjoy your family. I'll see you at work on Monday."

"You don't have to leave," she contended.

"Yeah, I think I do." He turned to Eldon. "I guess you can take it from here."

"Don't worry. She's in good hands," Eldon replied, sidling close to Catt. "Thank you for bringing our Catt back home and keeping her safe out there on the road."

"No problem."

Eldon draped his arm around Catt. "Come on, let's get you out of this rain." He ushered her toward the front door. Catt looked back at Jamal one last time before heading inside.

Jamal walked back to his car and was approached by Jeremiah. "I want to thank you again for looking out for my daughter," he told him.

"No problem, sir. It was my pleasure."

Jeremiah frowned a little at the remark. "You know, Mr. Ford, you don't see a lot of women like Catt anymore. She's a good girl. She loves the Lord, and she tries to do the right thing."

"I know," agreed Jamal. "That's what I respect most about her."

"That's good. While she's well-educated and all that, she hasn't had a lot of *worldly* experience, not the way you probably have."

Jamal listened, debating about whether he should be offended.

"A woman like Catt needs a special kind of mate, and I think she's found that in the minister. They're equally yoked. Do you know what that means?"

"Yes."

"Now, I'm not going to get into your business about anything that may or may not have happened out there on the road. That's between you and Catt. But she's home now. It's time to let things get back to normal. Do you know what I'm saying?"

He did and decided that he was offended. "It sounds like you're saying Catt is too good for me, or maybe I'm not good enough for Catt. Is that the gist of it?"

Jeremiah held up his hands a little. "Now, don't go taking this personally. But we both know that a man like you would never be serious about a woman like her. It doesn't have anything to do with who's too good for whom. It's about doing what's right. I know that my daughter has developed feelings for you, but what's *right* is that you step back and let her and Eldon have their space."

"What if that's not what Catt wants?"

"Son, I believe I know Catt a whole lot better than you do."

Jamal opened the door and climbed into the truck. "No offense to you, Pastor, but truth be told, you don't half know your daughter at all."

Chapter 33

She had never given a man flowers, but nothing else about her relationship with Jamal had ever been conventional, so why should this be any different?

Catt hadn't seen or spoken to Jamal since he'd dropped her off that Friday evening. The two days of separation was long enough for her to realize two things: that she missed him terribly and that she was falling for him.

She'd wrestled with herself all weekend about whether to tell him. The risk of rejection was always hovering near, but so was the risk of missing out on happiness and sharing her life with the man who touched her in a way that had changed her forever.

Catt inhaled the bouquet of gardenias. She knew that he would smile the minute she presented them to him because he'd know that she was doing something for him that she'd never done for any other man walking the earth. It seemed apropos, considering that she'd never felt about another man the way she felt about him.

She imagined professing her affection for him and him sweeping her up in his arms in a grand romantic gesture. Eventually, he'd ask her to be his wife and she'd say yes. Then he'd kiss her, and they'd get married and have babies and build a house on the lake and adopt a dog named "Bullet" and be each other's reason for smiling. She visualized it all as she cradled the flowers in her arms and sauntered out to the car.

Of course, this was only fantasy. Real-life Jamal would probably make a bad joke and say something like, "I like you, but not as much as you like me," not meaning it a bit. She drove to work so full of hope and love that it never even occurred to her that he actually might not feel the same way.

Catt pulled open the glass doors of Telegenic and made her way past the empty lobby and darkened offices down to the lab.

Jamal was already there when she arrived. Just seeing him made her want to burst. She hid the flowers behind her back. "Hi, can I talk to you for a minute?"

"Only a minute," he answered without looking up from the papers he was shuffling on his desk. "I've got to meet with Oni and all the head honchos in about ten minutes."

She set the flowers down. "Should I come?"

"No need. I have all of our figures and stats typed up in this report. That's what most of my weekend was devoted to." He finally looked up. "How was your weekend?"

"Very restful. I actually got a chance to do some thinking."

"About what?"

"Just everything that's happened over the past few weeks."

"I'm sure if Minister Eldon has his way, the time you spent with me will be a mere blot in history."

Catt hesitated then blabbed, "Jamal, I think I might be falling in love."

Jamal studied her face. "You're serious, aren't you?"

She nodded. "I said *I think*. It's not official or anything."

"What about unofficially?"

She sighed. "Unofficially, it could be love."

"So there are still secrets between us after all," he feigned being heartbroken. "Between here and New York, I thought that we told each other everything."

"We did. I just didn't tell you this."

"So, what's the deal? Is it lust or the real thing?"

"Oh, it's definitely more than just lust. I really dig this guy, you know?"

"And he has no idea?"

"I haven't told him yet."

"Catt, if your feelings are this strong, you have to tell him."

"I don't think he could handle it. I know him. He'd just freak out and probably stop talking to me. He's a little on the neurotic side." Catt pretended to change her mind to make him press her for more details. "The more I think about it, the more I'm not so sure I should say anything. Telling him would just complicate things."

"Still . . . you should say something."

She moved closer to him. "Say what? That his smile is the first thing I think about when I wake up in the morning? That I miss him if I go even one day without talking to him? That a part of me has been crazy about him from the first day we met?"

"You should tell him exactly that. I know that it's a risk, but it's worth it. You never know—he might be feeling the same way."

"So, I should just come right out and say it just like that?"

"Yeah." He gathered his things for the meeting. "He'll probably be relieved that you told him. So will you."

"You really think so?"

"Have you ever known me to dole out bad advice? Please don't answer that!" They both laughed. "When are you going to confess your simmering passion to this lucky man of yours?"

She swallowed hard and looked him in the eyes. "I just did."

Jamal nodded and continued fussing with papers until he processed what he'd just heard. "What?"

Catt slid the report out of his hand and stood before him. "I said I just did. I think I'm falling for you, Jamal." She reached up and kissed him.

Jamal blinked back. "Um, was that for practice, to show me how you're going to act when you tell him?"

"No, that was the real thing."

"Catt, I . . ."

"You don't have to say anything," she assured him. "I'm not looking for it to be reciprocated or anything like that. I just want you to know how I feel."

He spoke tenderly. "No, I think I do need to say something . . . I mean, we're friends, Catt. When you told me you had fallen for someone, I assumed you were talking about the minister."

"Eldon's okay, but he's not the one my heart leaps for; it's you."

Jamal didn't say anything. Catt had expected him to be caught off guard, not somber, as he was now.

"Jamal, is everything all right?"

He exhaled. "Catt, there's something I need to tell you."

She braced herself. Either he was about to tell her he felt the same way, or he was going to break her heart.

"Do you remember Yvette? The woman who came in here that day?"

"Yes, what about her?"

"She and I . . ." His words trailed off. "Yvette's my girlfriend, Catt."

Catt almost choked. "*Girlfriend?* Since when?"

Jamal was tense. "We made it official this weekend."

"This weekend? Two days after you were trying to get me to sleep with you?"

"Catt, it wasn't like that—"

"It never is!" she shrilled. "And to think I almost gave in to you." She raised her hands in jubilance. "Lord, thank you for looking out for me when I'm too stupid to look out for myself!"

"Catt, this thing with Yvette started long before we set out on the tour. Don't turn this situation into a reflection of how I feel about you or what we've shared for the past three weeks. You know what that meant to me; you know what you mean to me, but . . ."

"But that was then, and this is now, right?" finished Catt. She shook her head. "This isn't right. You know it isn't."

"What's not right?"

"The way you tried to play me!" charged Catt.

He squinted his eyes. "*Play you?* After all this time, all we've said to each other, all we've done, how can you stand there and say I tried to play you?"

"You knew I had feelings for you, and you were perfectly willing to use them to your advantage if I'd let you."

"All I know is we were alone on the road for three weeks. When all you have is each other, it's easy to get caught up and think you feel something that isn't really there. I figured whatever you felt for me had an expiration date on it. Besides, your father made it very clear that he'd never approve of a relationship between us."

"My father?" she questioned, confused. "What does he have to do with it?"

"He pretty much told me that you and Eldon were destined for happily ever after and that I need not interfere with that. But that's not even the main issue. The point is that I'm with Yvette now."

Catt put her hands on hips. "Why? Did she make it through your precious thirty-Day Plan? Can you talk to her and share your deepest secrets with her like you can with me? Tell me, Jamal, what does Yvette have that I don't have?"

Jamal bit his lip, not saying anything. Then the truth dawned on her.

"Or maybe it's that I have something she doesn't have, like an extra hundred pounds," inferred Catt. "So the fat girl is good enough to tell your secrets to and sex up behind closed doors, but when it comes down to it, you want cute little arm-candy. It doesn't matter if she can't stimulate you outside of the bedroom; you gotta have the dime-piece who looks good enough to make *you* look good, not the one you have to explain why you're with."

Jamal ran his hands over his face. "Catt, I don't want you to think—"

"What don't you want me to think, Jamal? That I'm not special? That I'm not your *friend?*" She scooped up the flowers. "You can save it! I know I'm no super-model, but I know I've got a heck of a lot going for me than that panty-droppin' floozy you've decided to take up with. The fact that you couldn't look past my imper-fections to see the real me like I looked past yours to see the real you lets me know you don't even deserve to have a decent woman like me."

"I can't help what I am or what I'm not attracted to!" he protested.

"Oh, I get it, Jamal. I really do. Do you know why? Because I'm not attracted to weak, shallow, preten-tious, fake men like yourself! I'm fat, Jamal, not stupid, not undesirable, not ugly—just fat! I have feelings and contrary to what you may have heard, big girls *do* cry!" She thrust the flowers into his chest with tears burning in her eyes and ran out. She'd already let him see her vulnerable. It would be a cold day in hell before she let him see her cry over him.

Catt stormed out of the building, nearly crashing into Oni.

"Well, good morning to you too!" retorted Oni.

Catt grit her teeth. She had to repress her emotions until she was in the safety of her car. "Sorry, I didn't see you."

"I've been looking at some of the preliminary reports. The company execs have been very pleased with the work you and Jamal have been doing."

Catt barely muttered a quick, "Thank you."

"Don't be so excited, Catt." Oni peered at her with a raised eye. "Is everything all right?"

Catt sighed. "Jamal and I just had a disagreement, that's all."

"Is there some drama brewing between you two? You know we can't afford to have two of our best chemists at odds."

Catt waved her hand to dismiss him. "You know how he is."

"Yeah, I do. That's what concerns me."

"What do you mean?"

Oni took a deep breath. "I've had a strange feeling about some things . . ."

"About me and Jamal?"

She nodded. "Do you want to tell me about it? I'm not jealous if that's what you're worried about, but I am concerned."

"Don't be. There's nothing going on between us that will get in the way of work."

"Really? Because that's not what it looks like." Convicted, Catt stood silently. "Catt, can I be straight with you for a minute?"

"Go ahead."

"Look, I know that Jamal is charming and sexy and all those things that women think they want in a man, but he's also a lot of things they *don't* want too."

"Oni, I appreciate your concern, but I can handle Jamal."

"You see that's just it—I don't think you can." Catt's face turned to stone. "Now, don't get mad; just hear me out. Jamal may talk a good game, but he's never going to let you in. There's a wall built up around him that's so thick that it'll be a miracle if anyone can break through it. And I can look at you and tell that you've already fallen for him, but he's never going to give more of himself than he already has."

"I'm not falling for him, Oni," lied Catt.

"You may be telling yourself that to keep from getting hurt, but we both know the truth. Get out now while you can. You're not qualified to play these love games with him."

Catt was on the defensive. "And you are?"

"I knew at first glance what he was all about. I'm not some naïve little girl anymore and after going through two divorces—"

"Is that what you think—that I'm some lovesick moron who's gotten in way over her head?"

"That's not what I'm saying, Catt. I'm older than you and a lot more jaded. At this point in my life, I'm not looking for romance. I have a career that I'm trying to build, and that's my priority right now. For me, all I need is a piece here and there, and I'm out. But you, you still want the house and the kids, and there's nothing wrong with that. I just don't want you to put your hopes into having that with Jamal."

"I'm not. Just the other night, he confided some things to me that he hasn't told anyone. Throughout the whole trip, I thought I saw changes in him, but it wasn't real. The second we got back, he turned back into his same self-indulgent self."

"Catt, men like Jamal don't change overnight, if ever. I'm glad that the two of you shared a moment, but I'm mighty afraid that's all it was."

Catt's eyes swelled with the tears she was saving for the emotional breakdown in the car. "I can't believe I almost let myself be taken in by him."

Oni rubbed her back. "Don't do it to yourself, Catt. He's not worth it. Try to make something work out with that Eldon fellow. He seems like someone worth crying over. You work with Jamal and you have fun with him, but that's it," advised Oni. "Don't pin your hopes and your happiness on a man like Jamal Ford. The only one who's going to end up getting hurt is you."

Chapter 34

Jamal lay on the bed trying to make sense of things. Had he really played Catt? Did he set her up for disappointment by dropping his guard and letting someone get close to him? Did she overthink and romanticize their situation, or had he subconsciously given her false hope? He never made her any promises, nor did he proclaim to have feelings for her that didn't exist. She had to have known that a relationship between the two of them would never work. They were too different. It was a bitter pill to swallow, but the sooner she accepted things as they were and moved on, the better.

Yvette emerged from the bathroom of her apartment wrapped in a robe after taking a shower. She began brushing her long black tresses. Jamal watched her reflection in the mirror. Yvette was beautiful, sophisticated, and uninhibited. What more could he ask for?

He rose from the bed and stood behind her. He took the brush from her and began stroking her hair with it. "I love watching you brush your hair," he muttered softly to her. "You smell good too." He set the brush down and started rubbing her back.

Yvette closed her eyes and sighed. "What's gotten into you?" she asked surprised. "Not that I'm complaining."

"I've just been thinking about how lucky I am to have you." He swept her hair to her right shoulder, leaving the left exposed. Then he traced her neckline with his tongue.

She turned around and kissed him on the lips. "We're both lucky."

They were soon tangled in each other's arms, breathing heavily and moaning lustfully.

"Make love to me, Jamal," whispered Yvette between kisses. Jamal extended his hand to Yvette. She accepted it, and he led her to the bed. He stretched her out on the comforter and kissed her on her neck. He whispered her name and placed his moist, inviting lips on her body. She arched her back in elation and clamped her legs around his waist.

Jamal's mind began to swirl with images of Catt. He thought of their near-kiss in his lab. He shook his head to block out the image and kissed Yvette again.

As he was kissing Yvette, his mind oscillated back to the time he and Catt picnicked in the park. Yvette's fingers digging into his back reminded him of Catt and how she clung to him after telling him about the rape.

All of a sudden, Catt's presence was overwhelming him, suffocating him. He could smell her melon shampoo and the floral-scented perfume that she wore. He heard her laughter ringing in his ears and could see her smile. The more he tried to push her out of his mind, the more forceful the images charged into it. The lustful feelings that he had for Yvette began languishing. Yvette could sense the change in him.

"What's wrong? Did I do something?" she asked, concerned.

Jamal rose from her bosom. "It's not you, Yvette. I just have a lot on my mind."

She pulled up behind him. "I think we both know what you have on your mind," she purred.

He reached out and grabbed her hand. He kissed it and turned to face her. "I'm sorry, Yvette. I can't do this."

"Why not?"

He released a sigh. "It's complicated." Jamal slipped his shirt back over his head and sat on the bed.

"I don't understand. One minute you can't keep your hands off me and now *this?*"

"I don't think that we should rush into anything that we might regret."

"How could I ever regret making love to a man who's as handsome . . ." she kissed him on the cheek, ". . . sexy," she kissed his neck, "and as virile as you, huh?"

"We don't need to use sex to cover our relationship, and I don't want to lead you on. I know how that feels," he tacked on, remembering the way he treated Catt.

"It won't be like that. I just want to hold you and to remember what it's like to be in your arms like that again. We were apart for three whole weeks. Maybe if you allowed yourself to be with me, you'd realize that everything that you are looking for is right here."

Jamal was tempted. Yvette did look beautiful tonight, and he desperately wanted to get Catt out of his mind, but he knew that he'd have to deal with his feelings for her and everything that had transpired between them sooner or later. If nothing else, being with Catt taught him that he was better off facing things head-on instead of trying to suppress it or mask the problem. More than that, he realized that he couldn't use sex as a means of escape anymore.

"I can't. I'm sorry."

"But, Jamal, don't you want me?" she asked. She slid the robe off and let it dissolve into a satin puddle at her feet. "We've never had a problem in the bedroom before."

"It's not that simple, Yvette. This just isn't right."

Stung by the rejection, Yvette hastily put her robe on again. "Is there something, or perhaps *someone*, that I should know about?" she asked, aggressively tying the robe belt into a tight knot.

"Yeah," he declared. "Me! And until I feel close enough to you to trust you like that, we don't need to be together."

"Are you dumping me?"

"I'm saying that we both deserve better."

Yvette crossed her arms over her chest. "Jamal, did something happen on the trip with that woman? Is there more to all of this than you're telling me?"

"Yeah, something did happen," he admitted. "She changed me."

"So, you're choosing that fat whale over all *this?*" She shook her head. "You're an idiot, you know that? I can name at least ten people who'd kill to be with me."

"I'm glad you can." He snatched up his jacket. "But as for me, I only need one."

Chapter 35

"I came over as soon as I could."

Catt pulled him into an embrace. "I'm so glad you're here. Thank you for coming over."

"You sounded pretty down on the phone," said Eldon, making his way into Catt's living room.

Since he was a child, Eldon had heard repeated declarations of, "The Lord works in mysterious ways." Now, he had proof.

It hadn't even been seventy-two hours since he'd walked Catt into her house after her three-week trip. While her father had talked to Jamal outside, Eldon used the brief moment of privacy to try and sneak in a kiss. To his dismay, Catt rebuffed him, telling him that she only wanted to be friends.

Catt's rejection not only cancelled her out as his future wife, but also crushed his aspirations of becoming the lead servant at Faith Temple. He'd briefly considered resigning as the youth minister—no need to stick around and watch someone else take his rightful place at the helm once Jeremiah retired.

Then it happened.

Catt called him in tears, asking him to come over. Once he asked all the right questions, he concluded that she wasn't in any physical danger and deduced that it must be emotional. He couldn't have been more delighted! Her phone call was the sliver of hope he needed to get his plan back into action.

He made a quick stop to the liquor store on his way to Catt's house. With a little luck and a few drinks, he'd be on his way to fatherhood by the end of the night.

Eldon led Catt to the sofa and sat down next to her. "Now tell me what happened."

"Eldon, I made such a fool out of myself," she confessed.

"What did you do?"

"I told Jamal that I was falling in love with him."

Eldon was taken aback. "And are you?"

Catt buried her face in her hands. "I don't know. I'm just really confused right now."

"Since I'm here instead of Jamal and you're this upset, I take it he doesn't feel the same way."

"No, he doesn't," she confirmed to Eldon's delight. "To make matters worse, he admitted to me that he has a girlfriend."

"Oni?"

"No. I wouldn't have been as insulted if it were Oni. The girlfriend is some mindless bobblehead who looks good in a miniskirt. Apparently, that's one of his stringent requirements."

"He's a jerk, Catt. You're better off without him."

"I realize that now, but it still hurts," said Catt, her voice cracking from holding back tears.

"I know what you need." Eldon reached into the brown paper bag that Catt noticed him walk in with. He pulled out a bottle of Long Island Iced Tea. "It's your drink of choice, isn't it?"

Catt declined. "I'm feeling bad enough without adding a depressant to the mix."

"Come on, one drink isn't going to kill you. It might even make you feel better."

"I thought you didn't drink," recalled Catt.

"I didn't say I *never* have a drink. It's rare that I do, but it's been known to happen." He looked around the room. "Where do you keep your glasses?"

She pointed to the left. "They're in the kitchen."

"I'll be right back."

Eldon got up and returned with two iced glasses in hand. He set them down on the coffee table and filled them to the rim with liquor.

"You must be thirsty," hinted Catt.

"You're not the only one with problems. Drink up!"

"What happened to 'taking it to the Lord in prayer'?" asked Catt, lifting the glass.

"I do that, but I'm doing this while I wait for the answer." He tossed back the drink. Catt followed suit.

After the first drink, Catt was already feeling better. By the second, she was relaxed and giggling at everything Eldon said. By the third time he topped off her drink, she could barely walk from the living room to her bathroom. By the time they emptied the bottle, Catt was practically in a stupor and stretched out on the sofa.

"Catt?" he whispered. Eldon was still sober. He'd sipped from the same glass all night while continuing to ply Catt with drinks. "Can you hear me, Catt?"

She groaned and lay back with her eyes shut. Her left arm was lapped across her forehead.

"Are you feeling okay?"

She wiggled her fingers to let him know she heard him.

His eyes drifted over her body. She was wearing a skirt. He was glad; it would make his job a whole lot easier.

He groped her legs and ran his hand up her thigh. He waited for her to protest. She didn't. It would be easier than he thought.

He pecked her gingerly on the lips. "You're so beautiful, Catt. I waited a long time to be alone with you like this." He eased his hand up her blouse and unbuttoned the first few buttons.

The coldness of his fingers on Catt's bare skin roused her out of her semiconscious state enough to sense something was wrong.

"What are you doing, Eldon?" slurred Catt. She could feel the weight of his body on hers but lacked the strength to move him.

"Showing you how much I want you." He began kissing her again, forcing his tongue inside her mouth. He stopped kissing her long enough to reach for her panties.

The brief interruption gave her mind a second of clarity, and she grabbed his hand. "Wait a minute." She was breathing hard and had to catch her breath.

"Baby, don't talk." He covered her mouth with his, kissing her again.

She pulled away. "But we have to talk." She felt his hand under her skirt again. "Eldon, stop," she insisted, steering his hand away.

"Shhh . . . you don't have to say anything. I've got this."

Catt felt weak. "The room is spinning. I think I'm going to be sick."

Eldon lifted himself off of her a little. "Just relax. Take a couple of deep breaths." She obeyed. "You feel better?"

"Somewhat."

"Close your eyes." He pecked her lips. "You don't have to do anything, just lay there. I'll take care of the rest."

The drowsiness overtook her. She closed her eyes but couldn't muster the strength to even open them. She tried to speak, but it was no use.

Eldon climbed on top of her. "Now . . ." He kissed her again. "Where were we?"

It took all she had, but Catt managed to murmur, "We shouldn't be doing this . . ."

"Come on, Catt. You know you want it." He buried his face in her neck, passionately kissing her.

They were interrupted by pounding on the door. "Come on, Catt. It's me. Let me in!" called a muffled voice.

"Who is that?" asked Catt, barely above a whisper.

Eldon fumed and slid off of her. "Don't worry. I'll get rid of him." Eldon zipped his pants back up and answered the door.

Jamal was standing on the other side of it. "Where's Catt?"

Eldon bore holes into Jamal with his eyes. "She's busy."

"Can you tell her I need to talk to her? It's important."

"She doesn't want to talk. No, let me rephrase that: she doesn't want to talk to *you*."

"I want her to tell me that," barked Jamal.

"I don't think Catt wants any company right now, you know what I'm saying?" He buckled his pants. "She's getting *exactly* what she needs *from me*."

The indication made Jamal hot with fury. He shoved Eldon aside and barged in. "I need to talk to Catt."

"She doesn't wanna talk to you," reiterated Eldon. "I think it'll be best if you leave."

Jamal spotted Catt on the sofa with her blouse undone and her skirt pulled up. She appeared to be sleeping. He whirred around. "What's going on in here?" he demanded.

Eldon stood next to Catt. "What does it *look* like?"

Jamal picked up the empty bottle on the coffee table. "How much did she have to drink?"

"One or two drinks, why?"

Jamal kneeled down beside her. "Catt?" He shook her a little. "Catt, can you hear me?" She responded with a moan.

"Leave her alone," ordered Eldon. "Can't you see she doesn't want to be bothered?"

"I'll believe it when she tells me that." Jamal lightly tapped her on the face. "Catt?"

Jamal's mind flashed back to Catt's confession about the rape and subsequent abortion. The scene mirrored the one Catt had described to him. She was on the sofa passed out after having too much to drink with a man who was obviously trying to take advantage of her inebriated state. He couldn't help her then, but he could definitely save her now.

Jamal looked up at Eldon, his eyes filled with rage and disgust. "You call yourself a preacher? How could you do this to her?"

"Catt didn't do anything she didn't want to do," he insisted.

"Are you kidding me? She's not even awake!"

"What did I do that you didn't try to do while you were out there on that road, huh?"

"The difference is that I never had to get her drunk to do it."

"Maybe you should've."

The insinuation incensed him. Jamal rose and socked Eldon squarely in the mouth with all the force he could assemble. Caught unawares, Eldon stumbled back and pressed his hand against his busted lip to neutralize the pain. Blood dribbled down his chin.

"Now, you can walk out, or I can send you flying out!" threatened Jamal. "Better yet, why don't I just call the police and let them do it. Explain to them why Catt is like this."

If nothing else, Eldon knew when to give up a losing battle. "You know what—all y'all are crazy! I don't need this!" He swung the front door open and stomped out into the night.

Jamal tried to raise Catt's head. "Catt, sweetie, sit up. Can you do that for me?"

"I'm too dizzy," she moaned.

"Okay, just lie here then." He pulled her skirt down. "Are you all right?"

Her eyes sprung open. "Where's Eldon?"

"He left. Did you have any idea what was going on?"

She exhaled deeply. "We had something to drink," she recalled. "And he was all over me. I tried to get him to stop. I just couldn't."

"It looks like I got here just in time. That guy is never going to bother you again, Catt. I'll make sure of that."

She closed her eyes. "Okay." Sleep overtook her again.

Jamal hunted for two blankets in Catt's linen closet. He found a quilt and an old comforter. He spread the quilt out over her body and made a pallet for himself on the floor next to the sofa. He was determined to stay as long as it took to make sure she was safe.

Chapter 36

Catt woke up to find Jamal in her kitchen brewing coffee. She didn't remember when he got there. More important, she couldn't remember *why* he was there.

Jamal noticed that she had stirred. "Good morning." He brought her a cup of coffee. "How do you feel?"

She sat up. "Confused. What's going on?"

"What do you remember about last night?" He sat down on the edge of the couch.

"It's spotty. I know Eldon was here, and that we had a few drinks." She stretched her brain to recall more details. "I don't really remember too much after that. When did you get here?"

"Last night while Eldon was here."

She was still confused. "Why did you come?"

"I had something I wanted to tell you. It's a good thing I got here when I did, though."

"Why?"

Jamal hesitated, not wanting to upset her. "Things were getting out of hand with Eldon."

"What do you mean?"

Jamal reached out to her. "When I got here, you were practically passed out and he . . ."

Catt swallowed hard. "He what?"

"Your shirt was undone, and your skirt was pulled all the way up. I think he was trying to . . . It looked like he was about to rape you."

Catt stopped him. "No, not Eldon. He wouldn't do anything like that! You must be mistaken."

"I don't think so, Catt. He was trying to take advantage of you. He didn't even deny it."

"He didn't?"

Jamal shook his head. "If I hadn't come over, I'm truly afraid of what would've happened."

Catt was thoughtful, quiet. "I trusted him. I thought he was my friend."

"He talks a good game, but he's a snake, Catt."

"When I think about all the lives he's been put in charge over . . . he's the *youth* minister, for Christ's sake!"

"I just hope he doesn't have the nerve to show his face around here again."

"I can't believe this is happening to me again." Catt was utterly distraught. "How could I be that stupid? After everything that happened before, you'd think I would know better by now."

"Don't do that, Catt. Don't start blaming yourself! This guy had you so drunk that you would've consented to anything. And it's not like it was before. I got here before he could really do anything."

"I can't thank you enough for saving me." She raised her eyes. "I can't thank God enough for sending you when He did."

"God might not be that pleased with me. When I realized what Eldon was up to, I decked him pretty hard."

Catt broke into a smile. "I'm sure God'll overlook it under the circumstances."

"Yeah, let's hope so!"

"You never did tell me what the reason was that you came over."

Jamal shook his head. "We don't need to get into that right now."

"But I want to. For you to come across town in the middle of the night, it must've been important."

"Are you sure?"

"Yes, did something happen at work?"

"This wasn't about Telegenic. It's about us."

"What about us?"

He stood up. "I felt very bad yesterday after the way things went down with us."

She sighed. "Jamal, you don't have to apologize. I realize now that I saw and believed what I wanted to. You were honest with me about who you were and what you wanted from the get-go. I should've listened."

"I may have been honest with you, but I wasn't honest with myself," he admitted.

"How so?"

"After you left yesterday, it dawned on me how much our friendship means to me. The thought of you not being a part of my life hit me like a ton of bricks. Catt, I can't imagine waking up and not being about to see you or talk to you again. I can't even think about it."

"You'll get over it. You managed just fine without me before we met."

"And that's all it was—*managing*. With you, I feel like I'm *living*. I'm not ready to let that go. I'm not ready to let *you* go. Catt, you have no idea what you mean to me."

She sat upright. She could see the sincerity in his eyes. "You're serious, aren't you?"

"Do you remember asking me if I was happy?" She nodded. "Catt, the only time I can truly remember being happy within the past few years is when I've been with you." He squeezed her hand. "Maybe it's our time to see what this thing is between the two of us."

"Geez, Jamal, if I didn't know any better, I'd think you were in love with me," she joked. Jamal looked solemn and didn't respond. "I was kidding, Jamal. I know that you're not in love with me." She saw how serious he looked. "Or *are* you?"

"What do you think?"

"I can't tell," she said slowly, thrown by his intense stare, "especially not with you acting and looking at me the way you are right now."

"What would you say if I said that I *am* in love with you?"

"I don't know. I guess I'd have to be in that situation."

He paused. "You *are* in that situation."

"What situation is that? I need to hear you say it."

Jamal took a deep breath. "I have to admit it. I think I love you, Catt. I know that this wasn't anything we planned on, but it happened."

Catt wasn't sure how to respond. "How long have you felt this way? When I came to you yesterday and told you how I felt, you said all you could ever see me as is a friend."

"I think I felt it all along; I just didn't want to admit to you or to myself." He touched her face. "In the beginning, I thought that you were just like everyone else. That's why I treated you like that. But as we started getting to know each other, I began to feel things that I thought were dead inside of me. I was hopeful and happy again. I started to trust and feel like I was capable of loving someone other than myself. You did that for me, Catt, and I will always be grateful for it."

"Gratitude isn't the same thing as love, Jamal."

"What I feel for you is more than just gratitude. I hope you give me a chance to prove it."

She looked away from him. "I don't know."

"You don't know what? Are you going to sit here and try to convince me that you don't feel anything for me?"

She carved her initials into the sofa with her finger. "You know I do, but it's complicated. I'm not trying to get hurt again."

"Catt, I know men like Eldon and Greg have hurt you, but it won't be like that with me. I'm not them."

She stared him down. "Jamal, this isn't about them. *You're* the one who hurt me! I thought after all we'd said to each other and been through, that you finally saw the real me, and you accepted me just as I am." She dropped her head. "But you didn't. Let me tell you something, Jamal. I like myself. I love my body. Yeah, I know I could stand to lose a few pounds, but so could you. And you know what? One of your eyes is higher than the other, and you have an overbite, and you have small little monkey hands, and you can't dance. I could go on about all the things wrong with you, but I didn't care. I saw past all that to the heart."

"I see that too," he argued.

"Yeah, now, but you chose Yvette over me. You knew that she wasn't the one, but she was pretty and you wouldn't have to explain to your boys why you were with her. You're shallow, Jamal, and I don't want a man like that."

"You won't even give us a chance?" he asked.

"You wouldn't give us a chance, Jamal. I'm top choice, not second best."

Jamal could say nothing.

"For the record, I'll always be grateful for the time we spent getting to know each other crisscrossing the country, and God knows I thank you for coming to my rescue last night. But as far as anything else goes, that ship has sailed."

He rose, humbled and heartbroken. "I appreciate your honesty, Catt, and I respect your decision. You're right. I should've seen what was right in front of me, but I didn't. It's a mistake that I'll probably regret for the rest of my life."

She stood up to walk him out the door. "I guess I'll see you at work."

"Are you going to be okay here by yourself?"

"Yes," she stated with finality, and she knew in her heart she actually would be.

Chapter 37

Jeremiah was seated at his desk confounded and holding a letter when Catt found him.

"I just don't understand it," he told her. "When I got here this morning, I found this letter taped to my door. It's from Minister James. He just up and quit with no explanation other than this isn't the church where the Lord wants him to be."

Catt sat down. "Have you heard from him?"

"No, have you?"

Catt shook her head. "I don't expect to either, not before we get a court date."

Jeremiah reeled back. "A court date?"

"I'm pressing charges against him. Daddy, last night, Eldon tried to rape me."

"What?"

"It's true, and if Jamal hadn't showed up when he did, Eldon might have been successful."

"Oh, baby girl . . ." Jeremiah rose and hugged his daughter. "Why didn't you call me? You know I would've dropped everything to come be with you. I'm so sorry this happened to you."

She released him. "I'm all right, Daddy."

"Well, come on. Let's go on down to the police station. I want him found and locked up today!"

"Thank you for offering, but this is something I want to handle on my own. I can't keep depending on you to come to my rescue whenever I get into trouble. That's what the Lord is for."

"I still wish you had called." Jeremiah's nostrils flared. "Boy, if I ever get my hands on that imp—" He closed his eyes and recited, "'Vengeance is mine,' said the Lord."

"I have to accept my responsibility in all this too," confessed Catt. "I never should've been drinking with him. I know my limits, and I allowed myself to go past them. It still doesn't justify what he did, but if I hadn't been so out of it, things never would've gotten that far." She stood firm. "You've got to accept your part in it too."

"What do you mean?"

"Daddy, you practically gift wrapped me for Eldon. I told you I wasn't interested, but you insisted on imposing your will over mine and God's. He's a monster, and this is the man you had picked out for me to marry!"

"Catt, if I had any inkling that he was capable of something like this, I never would've allowed him into this church, much less near my only child. I thought he was a good man and that he'd make a good husband for you."

Catt raised her voice. "Don't you see? That's not your decision to make. It's mine!"

"You're right," he conceded. "You're going to have to forgive me, sweetheart. As a father, I only want the absolute best for my daughter. I want to know that I'm leaving you in the hands of a man who'll love you as much as I do. Obviously, I went overboard this time."

"You go overboard *every* time! You don't have to find a husband for me, Daddy. I'm perfectly capable of finding a man on my own."

"I know that. I just hate to see you all alone."

"I'm alone by choice, and there's a difference between being alone and being lonely. Yes, I would like to get married someday, but I'll be all right if it doesn't happen."

"I never want you to underestimate how special you are just because some of these men out here are too fool-headed to recognize it."

"Why wouldn't they recognize it, Daddy? Come on, just say it."

"What are you talking about?"

"The reason you don't think I can find a man and why you feel the need to do it for me is because I'm fat, right?"

"Catt, I think you're the most beautiful, smart, virtuous woman I've ever met!"

"But fat, though, correct?" Jeremiah pressed his lips together. "Daddy, the only time I feel bad about my weight is when *you* make me feel bad about it! I see how you look at me if I get an extra helping at dinner or if I skimp on working out. The weight makes you far more uncomfortable than it makes me. I'm not worried about my size keeping me from finding a man. Not all women feel they need a man to validate them. I like myself just fine. If the man comes along, that's icing. If he doesn't, I'm still the whole cake just being me."

"I just worry about you, baby girl. I'm a parent, it's my job."

"Your job is to pray for me and put it in the Lord's hands."

Jeremiah folded his hands together. "Catt, you remember all those years ago, when your mother was on drugs?"

"Yes."

"A part of me always felt like things got so bad because I didn't do all I could to protect her. I guess that's why I work so hard at protecting you. I'm not worried about you getting into drugs or anything like that, but I see you killing yourself with food and it scares me. I'm not always going to be around to look after you, but

I can rest easy knowing that you have someone who will."

Catt kissed her father on the cheek. "I love you, and I love you for being concerned. But, Daddy, I'm a grown woman. At some point, I've got to start taking care of myself, and you've got to let me do that. I can't be your baby girl forever."

"If I promise to stop meddling in your life, will you be my baby girl for five more minutes?"

Catt smiled and slid into her father's arm. She was a woman now, but it did feel good to be Daddy's little girl one more time.

Chapter 38

"You know they're talking about giving you a raise," touted Jamal the second Catt stepped off the elevator and into the laboratory. It was refreshing to see him standing there. "The shot-callers are so impressed with the work we did on the road, they want to give us more money."

Catt smiled modestly. "Hey, if they want to give me more money, who am I to stop them?"

"Oni says they're even talking about sending us to our markets on the West Coast. Would you be willing to go back out on another adventure with me?"

She frowned. "I'd have to do some serious thinking and praying about that one. You know what happened the last time we traveled together."

"The last time, we got to know each other as individuals. This time, we can get to know each other as a couple."

"That's not going to happen, Jamal." She noticed he was tinkering with some of the test tubes. "You working on the next masterpiece over there?"

He poured liquid into a test tube. "I'm trying to. Here, smell."

She took a whiff. "That's nice. It's sexy."

"It's called Chase. All the ladies want to be chased, right?"

"Some do. Others like to be caught."

"Which one are you?"

Catt eased into her lab coat. "The data is inconclusive."

Jamal abruptly grabbed her and pulled Catt to him. "If I apologized to you a thousand times for being an idiot for choosing Yvette over you, would there be a chance for us?"

"Jamal, why are you doing this?"

"Because I need to know. My whole future is at stake here."

"Then the answer is no."

"So, you're not willing to give us a try?"

"Jamal, I can't, not with everything that's going on right now."

"Catt, what if we're throwing away our last chance at real love? We have to at least try."

"I believe that if things are meant to be, they'll be. If it's meant for us to be together, we'll find our way back to each other. And it'll be real—not because I'm confused or on the rebound or because you're trying to run away from your problems."

"You said that you loved me."

"I do, but can you promise me that if Yvette or some other emaciated model walked through this door right now and begged you to take her home you wouldn't do it? I don't think you can, and I deserve better than that."

"You do deserve better, and I can honestly say that I'm willing to do whatever it takes to prove to you that I can be the kind of man you deserve. I want to be the kind of man God wants me to be for you. And I feel in my gut if we don't give ourselves another chance, we'll regret it for the rest of our lives."

She squeezed his hand. "I hear what you're saying, Jamal, and it means the world to me that you'd put your heart and pride on the line this way, but right now, I've got to do what's best for me. You understand that, don't you?"

She turned away and walked into her office, vindicated. Yes, Jamal was finally saying all the things that she'd longed to hear, but her heart wasn't ready to go there with him. For all she knew, he was just caught up in his emotions for the moment and would change his mind again before she could blink twice. Perhaps he felt guilty for leading her on or felt the need to protect her from the likes of men like Eldon. Didn't he know she was fully capable of taking care of herself, and even if she wasn't, God was?

Then again, for all she knew, he just might have meant it when he said he loved her, and it had nothing to do with feeling obligated or guilty or the need to protect her. And for all she knew, Jamal Ford just might be the one. Even if he wasn't, it was worth a shot, right?

Catt peeked out of her office at Jamal tending to the beakers. He *was* fine, and there were definitely worse ways to spend her summer than traveling with the man she adored.

A minute later, Catt joined Jamal in the lab with a smile on her face. "So . . . when do we leave for Cali?"

Reader Discussion Questions

1. Do you think that Catt being overweight is significant to the story, or would the book have had the same impact regardless of her size? Explain.

2. Is Catt genuinely a spiritual person, or does she use religion as an excuse to isolate herself and to avoid dealing with her problems?

3. Do you think Eldon was sincere about his feelings for Catt, or was she just a pawn in his pursuit of becoming the pastor of Faith Temple?

4. Should Jeremiah have accepted some of the blame for Catt's near-rape by Eldon? Why or why not?

5. Do you think Jamal's spiritual transformation is real, or was he just caught up in the moment or succumbing to pressure from Catt?

6. Is Jeremiah controlling, or does he simply want what's best for his daughter? Does he seem spiritually grounded enough to pastor a church?

7. If you were in Catt's position at the time, would you have aborted your child? Why or why not?

Reader Discussion Questions

8. Should Catt have taken Jamal back after he rejected her because of her weight? Why or why?

9. Which character do you think evolved the most by the end of the story? How so?

10. Do you consider Catt and Jamal to be "equally yoked" to each other? Why or why not?

Urban Christian His Glory Book Club!

Established in January 2007, *UC His Glory Book Club* is another way to introduce **Urban Christian** and its authors. We are an online book club supporting Urban Christian authors by purchasing, reading, and providing written reviews of the authors' books. *UC His Glory Book Club* welcomes both men and women of the literary world who have a passion for reading Christian-based fiction.

UC His Glory Book Club is the brainchild of Joylynn Jossel, author and Executive Editor of Urban Christian and Kendra Norman-Bellamy, author and copy editor for Urban Christian. The book club will provide support, positive feedback, encouragement, and a forum whereby members can openly discuss and review the literary works of Urban Christian authors. In the future, we anticipate broadening our spectrum of services to include online author chats, author spotlights, interviews with your favorite Urban Christian author(s), special online groups for *UC His Glory Book Club* members, ability to post reviews on the website and amazon.com, membership ID cards, *UC His Glory* Yahoo! Group and much more.

Even though there will be no membership fees attached to becoming a member of *UC His Glory Book Club,* we do expect our members to be active, ted, and to follow the guidelines of the book c

UC His Glory Book Club members pledge to:

- Follow the guidelines of *UC His Glory Book Club*.

- Provide input, opinions, and reviews that build up, rather than tear down.

- Commit to purchasing, reading, and discussing featured book(s) of the month.

- Respect the Christian beliefs of *UC His Glory Book Club*.

- Believe that Jesus is the Christ, Son of the Living God.

We look forward to the online fellowship.

Many Blessings to You!
Shelia E. Lipsey
President
UC His Glory Book Club
**Visit the official Urban Christian His Glory Book Club website at:
www.uchisglorybookclub.net